PSYCHOPOMP

Books by Angela Roquet

Lana Harvey, Reapers Inc.
Graveyard Shift
Pocket Full of Posies
For the Birds
Psychopomp
Death Wish
Ghost Market
Hellfire and Brimstone
Limbo City Lights (short story collection)
The Illustrated Guide to Limbo City

Return to Limbo City (A Lana Harvey Spin-off Series)
Life After Death
Shadow of Death

Blood Vice
Blood Vice
Blood and Thunder
Blood in the Water
Blood Dolls
Thicker Than Blood
Blood, Sweat, and Tears
Flesh and Blood
Out for Blood

Spero Heights
Blood Moon
Death at First Sight
The Midnight District

Haunted Properties: Magic and Mayhem Universe
How to Sell a Haunted House
Better Haunts and Graveyards
This Old Haunt

Visit **angelaroquet.com** for a complete list of Angela's works.

PSYCHOPOMP

LANA HARVEY, REAPERS INC.

BOOK FOUR

ANGELA ROQUET

VIOLENT SIREN PRESS

PSYCHOPOMP

Copyright © 2014 by Angela Roquet

This is a work of fiction. Names, characters, places, and incidents either are the product of the author's imagination or are used fictitiously. Any resemblance to actual events or locales or persons, living or dead, is entirely coincidental.

www.angelaroquet.com

Cover Art by Rebecca Frank

Edited by Chelle Olson of Literally Addicted to Detail

ISBN: 978-1-951603-01-4

For my mama.
She didn't like that Gabriel was a drunken bum.
It's her fault that he's a more upstanding citizen
these days.

CHAPTER ONE

"An education isn't how much you have committed to memory, or even how much you know. It's being able to differentiate between what you know and what you don't."
—Anatole France

The entrance essays for the demon defense course Bub would be teaching at the academy this semester were deplorable. I'd learned that word from Jack, Bub's butler, but I'd figured out the definition all on my own. It meant that they were shit.

I threw the latest disasterpiece down on Bub's desk. "Why am I helping you review these again?"

Jack slipped off his reading glasses and rubbed the small span of forehead between his gritty horns before pinching the bridge of his nose. "Because you're more familiar with this bilge that your kind mistakenly calls English. And Master Beelzebub insisted that you approve the class roster."

"At this point, he's more likely to have an apprentice than a class." I slouched back in my chair and gazed out the darkened window of Bub's study.

It was well after nine. The light was fading behind the mountains, leaving only a thin line of pink along the sharp skyline. Bub still hadn't returned from his meeting with the Hell Committee.

Jack followed my eyes to the window and sighed. "I think we've tortured ourselves enough for one night. Would you care to join me for tea and dessert?"

I was still full from the dinner Jack had prepared—that Bub had also missed—but I nodded anyway. Sugar would help ease my disappointment. Besides, Jack made a chocolate mousse that was to die for.

Bub's country home in Tartarus was swanky, but it was rustic and small enough to pass as charming. Well, except for the study. That room was downright archaic. I felt my shoulders sag with relief as we left the soaring shelves of volumey texts behind.

Clusters of antlers were fashioned into little chandeliers down the hallway, and they flamed to life as we made our way toward the kitchen. I had a feeling it was more sorcery than modern technology, but Bub was known to dabble in both.

We bypassed the dining hall, opting for the humble breakfast area in the main kitchen. Between the cooling ovens and low ceilings, the room was toasty. The stone floors were polished to a shiny gray. They matched the alcove shelving behind the counter that dissected the room, separating the old table from the modern gadgets in the otherwise medieval kitchen.

I took a seat while Jack paused at the pantry to slip an apron over his dapper butler attire. It was a simple white garment, but it managed to look comical on the stuffy old demon. I pressed my lips together in an effort to hide my grin.

"What?" Jack blinked stiffly.

"I'm just excited to try your chocolate mousse."

Jack raised an eyebrow before clearing his throat and setting to work, retrieving a carton of cream from the refrigerator. He poured some into a metal bowl and set it under an automatic mixer, quickly moving to the sink, where a basket of fresh berries waited in a colander.

Jack's forehead crinkled as he rinsed the fruit. "Unfortunately, the only decent essay I've read thus far happens to be the one submitted by your apprentice, Mr. Kraus, and he's least likely to need a formal education in demon defense, as he has you for a mentor."

"Kevin submitted an essay?" I frowned.

Why hadn't he told me? I'd been teaching him bits of what I'd learned over the summer, but I had to admit, I'd left out the more tedious lessons. I was just so relieved to be finished with my training and classes at the academy—and excuse me for not missing the migraines. Summer was meant to be enjoyed. I'd try harder now that fall was creeping up on us.

The mixer chimed as fluffy white peaks began to curl up out of the bowl. Jack retrieved the chocolate mousse from the refrigerator. He had made it right before dinner and left it to chill as a bribe to lure me into the study to read essays. Sneaky, old demon.

Jack placed three crystal serving glasses on the counter and put a healthy scoop of mousse in the bottom of each. Then he layered in the fresh whipped cream and spiraled the last of it on top for good form, outlining the rim of each glass with the berries. There was nothing Jack made that didn't look as wonderful as it tasted.

He picked up one of the glasses and sighed. "I'll set this one in the chiller for Master Beelzebub."

"I think not, good sir." Bub suddenly appeared in one of his flashy business suits. It was a shiny blue number with a gold tie that matched the flecks swirling in his dark irises. He slipped out of his jacket and flung it over his shoulder before taking the dessert from Jack.

Jack handed the remaining glass of mousse to me and took his own down the hall with a huff. I think he had been looking forward to discussing the essays further, but I couldn't say that I wasn't relieved to have that conversation postponed. I also couldn't say that I wasn't relieved that Bub had finally shown up. I felt a little pathetic that I had waited around so late, hoping to see him. I could feel my skin warm from embarrassment. Bub did his best not to gloat, but I could see it in his tired eyes all the same.

"How'd the meeting go?" I asked.

He tossed his jacket over a chair and joined me at the table. "Same trouble in paradise, different day."

"Well. That's nice and vague, and it perfectly explains why you're nearly three hours late." I peeled my eyes away from him and took a bite of mousse.

Bub had the decency to look ashamed. "It was a horribly long meeting, about horrible people with horrible plans. Please, forgive me for not wanting to relive the tedious details a second time in one evening. I have better things in mind."

The twinkle returned to his eyes as he dropped his gaze to take in the low cut of my dress. It felt a little wasted at this hour.

"Your better things will have to wait. I've already stayed longer than I should have. Jack asked me to go over the entrance essays for your class." I raised an eyebrow.

Bub chuckled nervously. "I've read some of them. I asked Jack to help out a little. After all, what are butlers for?"

"You have to turn in an approved list by Friday. You do realize that's in two days, right? Have you even started on your lesson plans, or is Jack doing that, too?"

"Lana." His shoulders slumped. "I know I play the part of a carefree socialite, but try to keep in mind that I actually do have actual responsibilities." His face creased, and he looked away. "I imagine they're not as legitimate as the likes of Maalik's."

"Not that again," I groaned. "He had the Helm of Hades. I had a plan, and it went all to hell when he was injured—"

"*I'm* able to achieve invisibility without the helm. You could have included *me* in the plan." Bub's brows pinched together in hurt confusion.

"We've been over this." I raked a hand through my curls. "You're the better warrior, and you obviously know more about demon defense. You're teaching a class on it."

"Right." He pushed his half-eaten dessert away. I knew Jack would be insulted, but I didn't feel like eating the rest of mine either.

"It's late. I should go."

Bub reached across the table and took my hand. "Let's not end our evening on a sour note, love," he said, amping up the charm with his English accent.

I placed my other hand on top of his. "How about a do-over? Friday night?"

He grinned and gave me a nod. "It's a date. I'll pick you up at seven."

I gave him a peck on the cheek and scooped up my glass of mousse. "I'm taking this to go. Tell Jack I'll return the glass this weekend," I said with a wink.

I left through the foyer and stepped out onto the front lawn—if you could call parched desert a lawn—and coined myself back to the harbor of Limbo City.

Normally, I wouldn't have felt safe on the dock at night in nothing but my skimpy evening attire. But since Grim had deactivated coin travel through the city and installed nephilim guards at the travel booths, I didn't have to worry as much. Aside from the time Loki had shape-shifted into a guard and knocked me out cold, I hadn't had any problems with the new system. *It* was just that once, I reminded myself as I eyed the two guards standing watch at the end of the dock.

I made my way to the harbor travel booth and took it to the one across from Holly House. The city was cooler than Tartarus, and I shivered as my skin puckered with goose-bumps. A light fog wove its way through the courtyard and past the gates of the holiest abode in Limbo. A few months before, I had been slumming it in a crummy studio apartment, until a fire demon remodeled the place for me. It had taken a while to warm up to the ritzy new digs, and the ritzy new rent bill, but the added security was worth it.

I passed a gurgling holy water fountain and a few concrete angels on my way to the front door, where I paused to punch my security code into the cross-shaped box anchored to the stone wall. Charlie, the perpetually chipper deskman, called out a friendly greeting as I waited for one of the elevators. I gave him a short wave and smiled as one chimed open to take me to the tenth floor.

On the way up, I finished my chocolate mousse. I had three roommates, which meant nothing in the refrigerator was sacred. Chances were, everyone was sleeping soundly by now, but Josie and Kevin were usually up a bit earlier than I was. They were really taking advantage of the amenities at Holly House, especially the fully equipped gym. Jenni woke earlier than I did too, but not by much. Though punctuality was higher on my priority list now that I was captain of the Posy Unit.

The condo was dark and quiet, except for the grumbling snores of my hellhounds drifting down the hallway. I considered it comforting white noise, but I was pretty sure most people would find it as soothing as snuggling up with a couple of chainsaws.

I set my dessert glass in the sink and headed back to my bedroom. My mind was still on Bub. The fact that I still held on to some of my secrets hung in the air between us more and more lately. It wasn't like him to push or beg, and I hadn't noticed until recently that he was biding his time, waiting for me to unravel my mysteries to him. He already knew too many of my deepest and darkest for my comfort.

The secret that clearly weighed on Bub's mind the most these days was why I had asked him to fetch Maalik for me during the battle when we rescued Jenni Fang, my roommate and Grim's new second-in-command. The Helm of Hades, better known as the Cap of Invisibility, was a weak excuse, and I knew it. But it wasn't like I could come right out and say what he wanted so desperately to know.

Maalik was one of three people who knew the location of the secret Throne of Eternity—Grim and I being the other two. Winston, the former soul on the throne, had given Maalik a coin that would take him to the secret pocket realm from anywhere in Eternity. He'd given me one too, but after an impromptu abduction, Caim and Loki had relieved me of mine.

That's why I'd needed Maalik. The battle had beaten us down, and we were on the waning end of it. Maalik was our only hope for reinforcements. He went to Winston and gave him our coordinates, along with a request to activate coin travel in the cave corridor just beyond the battle and to level the main hall full of raging rebels. By some strange magic, we managed to escape.

Maalik hadn't even received proper thanks for the feat since not even Grim knew about the coins Winston had given us. The cave-in was written off as a fortunate coincidence. Everyone at the scene had been so relieved, that they hadn't thought to ask why or how coin travel had been activated within the cave corridor. Maalik and I were the only ones privy to that detail. It didn't mean that we were on our way to a tender reunion.

I could understand Bub's concerns, but I wasn't about to spill my guts to ease his mind. I was hoping a little time and attention would be enough to prove to him that I wasn't going anywhere. I was pretty smitten with the Lord of the Flies.

I still had some lingering questions about Maalik. For starters, I wanted to know if he was aware that in order to get us out of the cave alive, Winston had stepped down from the throne and installed the new soul I'd brought him as backup.

I wasn't sure how I felt about Naledi yet. She definitely wasn't Winston, but she did distract him enough that he didn't require my attention as frequently. In fact, I hadn't seen him since our follow-up meeting after the cave incident. It had been three weeks, and I still didn't have a replacement coin or any other means of contacting Winston. I was starting to get a little unnerved. If he didn't show soon, I'd have to suck it up and ask Maalik for an update. I was not looking forward to that conversation.

As far as I knew, Maalik didn't know that I had been commissioned by Horus to find backup souls for the throne. That was a secret I had guarded fiercely, and one that probably had more to do with our breakup than I cared to admit.

Maalik was good at his job on the council. Maybe too good. He wouldn't like what I was doing behind the scenes. I didn't really have a choice, though. Horus was prepared to expose my secrets to the council if I didn't help him relieve Winston of the throne. Now that Winston had stepped down, my task was essentially complete. Not that I could tell Horus that. Not yet, anyway.

Winston was in no hurry to leave the secret throne realm, and not just because he needed to keep up appearances with Grim for my sake. He was in love with the new soul. I hadn't been around them long enough to tell if Naledi returned the sentiment, but if she did, Horus might not be too happy at the end of his term when he fully expected Winston to follow him to Duat, the Egyptian afterlife.

Besides my mental turmoil, life had been simple for the past three weeks. The Posy Unit was running smoothly. Grim had been scarce. And best of all, Gabriel and I had patched things up.

My favorite archangel was living at Holly House now, and he was keeping his halo sharper these days, laying off the booze and mingling with political socialites. He'd even accepted a position on the Board of Heavenly Hosts.

Gabriel had taken a little longer to get past the rut we'd fallen into after the death of my mentor, Saul Avelo. But to be fair, I hadn't taken that first step willingly. We were both back on track now, and things were looking shiny.

⚒

CHAPTER TWO

"A friend is one who has
the same enemies as you have."
—Abraham Lincoln

Thursday morning started off as usual. I woke up feeling like death warmed over, probably because I didn't sleep in late anymore. I drank too much coffee with Jenni, and I fed the hounds so much Cerberus Chow that Saul's colon protested by filling the condo with noxious gas. Jenni left early. I heard her grumbling under her breath that she was lucky she hadn't eaten breakfast.

After the caffeine had kicked in, I showered and packed a fresh robe in my duffle bag. When Josie and Kevin returned from the gym, they took the hounds with them to our ship, while I checked in at the office to retrieve the harvest docket for the day.

Reapers Inc. headquarters was located on the seventy-fifth floor of the tallest building in Limbo City. The elevator ride only took about a minute and a half, but it felt like an eternity. The nameless minions responsible for maintaining the lobby had begun decorating for the fall, with frosted leaf garlands and wreaths, but the elevators were empty boxes of boredom. They seemed to serve as a reminder that this was not a place of cheer. The welcoming lobby was a cruel trick.

Ellen's face lit up when I stepped off the elevator. "Good morning, Ms. Harvey." She twitched excitedly in her chair behind the front desk, which had been adorned with a fall garland that matched the ones in the lobby.

"Hey, Ellen. Is it a good day to die?"

"As good as any other, I suppose. I put your docket on your desk." She grinned and rolled her eyes innocently toward the hallway. Ellen never left my soul docket in my office. She was also terrible at keeping her mouth shut.

I folded my arms and stared her down, refusing to beg, but also refusing to budge until she cracked.

Ellen huffed out an impatient sigh. "Oh, go see for yourself," she whispered, hopping up to follow me down the hall.

My desk had been transformed into a garden. Buckets of overflowing daisies sat in my guest chairs and along the windowsill. My mouth dropped open, and I quickly pulled Ellen into my office to close the door behind us.

"Grim is going to flip if he sees this."

Ellen giggled. "I'm surprised he hasn't followed his nose in here already. Don't they smell lovely?" She leaned over the desk, pretending to sniff the ripe blooms while stealing a peek at the note tucked inside the center bouquet. "They're clearly from your yummy demon prince. What's the occasion?"

"An apology, I'm guessing." I snorted and began moving the flowers from the guest chairs to the windowsill.

Ellen gasped. "What did he do?"

"He was three hours late for dinner." I shrugged. "Though it hardly seems to warrant all this."

Ellen tossed her manners and went ahead and plucked up the notecard. "*Looking forward to tomorrow night.* How dreamy." She held the card to her chest a moment before fanning herself with it. "Doesn't sound like an apology to me. More like a promise."

"Yeah, well, right now, I'd like someone to promise to help me move these out of here."

"I could sneak a few out when I head to lunch," she offered.

A light tap came at the door before Jenni Fang poked her head in. She took in the flowers with wide eyes. "I thought I smelled something. Do you have a minute, Lana?" She glanced at Ellen, who jumped and hurried to the door.

"I'll take care of as many of these as I can on my break," Ellen said before disappearing down the hall.

Jenni closed the door behind her and sat on the edge of my desk. She managed to make the casual act look more forced and uncomfortable than a chess team yearbook photo. Her once militant aura came off as too uptight and traumatized since her stint at the rebels' mercy. Instead, she had turned her personality inside out. The new, overly cheerful Jenni was so painfully obvious, it made me feel awkward for her.

I knew the behavior was expected. Survivors had to appear as though they had a new lease on life, lest everyone assume they were broken, haunted shells of who they once were. It wasn't fair, but life seldom was.

What bothered me the most about Jenni's newfound attitude was that she felt the need to keep up the façade for me, too. I was her roommate and one of her closest friends, as far as I could tell. Plus, I'd been on her rescue mission. I'd seen what she had been through. It didn't get uglier than that. If there was anyone she could let her walls down for, it was me.

Jenni cleared her throat and tried on a painful smile. "I have a lead on Caim," she said softly.

"That's great." I bit my bottom lip and tried to smile back.

"I'm sensing a but."

"But"—I nodded slowly—"are you sure you want to pursue it? Couldn't you send one of the Nephilim Guard units after him?"

Jenni's face creased despite her forced calm. "I could, but I don't want to. I want to make sure the job gets done right. I want to see his guts spill over my boots." Her voice dropped an octave. "I want to hold his head on a pike and parade it through his legions until the fight drains so completely from them that they never regain the will to rise in battle again."

"Okay there, Boudica." I shivered at her words even as I laughed. "Why are you telling me this?"

"Because I want you there with me."

"What?" I circled my desk and sat down. "Does Grim know about this?"

Jenni nodded. "He's approved you for a day off tomorrow."

"Tomorrow?" I squeaked. "Wow. That soon?"

"Can't risk the rebels moving." Jenni eased off my desk and began pacing. "Josie and Kevin will have to cover your workload, but we'll have Gabriel and Maalik with us, and they're better against demons anyway."

"We're not taking Josie and Kevin? Wait a minute. Maalik? And Gabriel? Have you spoken to them yet?"

Jenni whispered out a laugh. "No, actually. I wanted to tell you first." Her good mood seemed more genuine now, as if she had assumed I would refuse her.

Rushing into a nest of demons wasn't my idea of a good time, especially if Caim happened to be among them. It had been different when the goal was rescuing Jenni. But for revenge? I had my reservations. Still, after seeing what Caim had done to her, I could understand Jenni's thirst for vengeance, and I didn't have it in me to turn her down.

Josie wouldn't like being left out, and I had a feeling this was going to be one of those top-secret, shut-your-face kind of missions. The uneasy feeling in my stomach had more to do with Maalik, though. This was my chance to pump him for information and see what he knew about Winston and the throne. I was going to have to be careful about the way I approached him.

What I really needed was more time to think things over, and more time to see if Winston would come to me and save me from the confrontation with Maalik altogether.

Jenni stopped pacing and leaned over my desk. "I'm sure I don't have to tell you how confidential this mission is. Also, Grim's keeping it from the media, but another reaper has gone missing."

"What's that make? Three now?" I rubbed a hand over my forehead.

Jenni nodded. "It's Tasha Henry."

I sucked in a startled breath.

"Your generation, I know." Jenni touched my shoulder. "I'm so sorry. Were you friends?"

"Only during our initial schooling. It's just a little close to home, you know?"

"Yeah. Karen Durst wasn't much of a surprise after Miranda Giles, but I really didn't expect Tasha. I figured the rebels would be going after the more experienced reapers. No offense," she added quickly.

"None taken."

I was higher up the totem pole than most reapers my age. It was due more to crooked politics than my own ambition, but to my credit, I was doing a bang-up job.

Jenni resumed her pacing. "We really need to throw a wrench soon to discourage this trend. Hopefully, this lead will turn into a two birds-one stone operation. I'll have a file ready for you by the end of the day. I'll leave it on your desk." She paused as she reached my office door and looked over her shoulder, locking her dark eyes on mine. "Thank you, Lana."

"What are friends for?" *Apparently, suicidal revenge missions.*

Jenni's bright façade split, and for a brief second, her serious demeanor slipped between the cracks. "I mean it. There's no one else I'd rather have by my side when I take that bastard down. He took away everything, and you gave it back. Thank you."

She left my office in time to miss my doubtful expression. Caim and Loki had chained Jenni to a wall and tortured her for five days. When I found her, she was naked, bloody, and out of her mind. Cutting her free and putting a knife in her hand had conjured a second wind that made me never want to be on her bad side, but it certainly wasn't enough to erase the kind of scars she was trying like hell to hide.

I needed to push the mission out of mind and go over the harvests for the day, but Miranda Giles crept into my thoughts instead. She had been the first reaper to disappear after the rebels hiding in the city were busted last spring. She had also been Craig Hogan's girlfriend.

The bad taste that filled my mouth when I remembered the way I had reached into him and *literally* taken him out of existence hadn't paled. I imagined if Craig were still around, he would make a fourth missing reaper. He'd been working with the rebels before I *happened* to him. No one remembered Craig, except for me and Winston, who had been on the throne at the time—which seemed to make him eerily omnipresent.

The power to completely undo another being had been a nasty shock, but considering that it saved my ass, I couldn't complain too much. I wasn't yet used to the fact that I had the ability to see the potency of a soul, but to undo someone's entire existence? I didn't know—nor did I *want* to know—if Grim could do that, too. I had seen what he was capable of when he invited me to watch him torture Loki after his capture. The show felt more like a warning, and I'd been trying extra hard to mind my own business ever since. I didn't even have the nerve to approach him about the missing reapers.

The rumors flying around were petty goddess gossip. Some thought the MIA reapers were part of an underground association fighting for deityship rights that were hiding out in an afterlife or the mortal realm. Some had romantic notions that they'd run off with lesser deities. There were whispers of possible death or abduction by rebels, which was probably the best guess I'd heard so far.

The truth was a far messier business. The rebels weren't surprising us with the allies they managed to scavenge from the less-active afterlives, but recruiting reapers was a dirty move. A damn good dirty move. One less reaper meant more harvests that had to be distributed among the rest of us. It meant sloppier work and more chances to nab unattended souls, the underlying power source of Eternity. I imagine killing reapers would have worked just as well, but why kill a good soldier when you could lure them over to the dark side with promises of deityship and freedom?

I had my suspicions when Miranda disappeared right after the rebel bust in Limbo. Grim had put out a public notice, but he didn't bother to do the same for Karen. I had a feeling that he wouldn't even offer to comment on Tasha's absence. It didn't sit well with me that she was a member of my generation.

Of the six, eighth-generation reapers brought into existence in 1709, Vince Hare had been terminated for illegally selling souls on the ghost market, Craig Hogan had been zapped out of existence by yours truly, and now, Tasha Henry was missing. With my questionable promotions, my generation was turning out to be the most controversial lot of reapers of all time. It made me oddly nostalgic. If I survived Jenni's vengeance mission, I'd have to schedule a sit-down with the only two reapers left in my generation before they decided to make history, too.

CHAPTER THREE

"Seeing much, suffering much, and studying much,
are the three pillars of learning."
—Benjamin Disraeli

"It rhymes with moose. Try again."

Kevin jumped and looked over his shoulder. I'd just witnessed him arguing with the practice dummy on the poop deck of our ship. Apparently, the thing was refusing to burst into flames from his shoddy Latin.

Technically, the ship was mine and Josie's, but Kevin had been doing so much renovation work on it lately that it might as well have been his, too. Besides, he was my apprentice. For the next hundred years or so, what was mine was his—or something to that effect.

Kevin fiddled with the hem of his robe and ran a hand through his mess of hair. "Lana, I—"

"Seriously. Try again." I folded my arms and nodded at the dummy.

Kevin pressed his lips together and turned back to his target, lifting his palm outward. Sweat beaded on his crinkled brow as he inhaled deeply through his nose. "*Sanctus Incendia.*"

A thin line of smoke shot from his hand, along with a spark that flicked off the dummy like a cigarette butt. I couldn't quite tell if Kevin was more excited or disappointed by the improvement.

"Better," I said. "Come on. We'll have more time to practice later when we deliver our catch this afternoon."

"You're coming with us?" He cocked his head. "Don't you usually have paperwork at the office?"

"Yeah." I scowled. "I don't feel like dealing with Grim today. I'll drop off my reports after-hours."

I left off the bit about Bub dumping a greenhouse in my office. Kevin's lips were a little loose around Josie, and I didn't feel like playing twenty questions with her after work. I needed the time to go over Jenni's mission file, which I was doing my damnedest to push out of my mind for now.

Kevin bounced down the stairs beside me as we returned to the main deck for the morning meeting. "Sanctus, like moose," he repeated to himself with a nod and stuffed his hands into the pockets of his robe.

"Yeah, and in Latin, the *c* never makes an *s* sound. It's always pronounced like *cake*. That should help you fix *incendia*. You'll nail it later. Promise."

He gave me a skeptical smile.

The rest of the crew waited for us below. Kate Evans and Alex Grayson took turns tossing a ragged softball down the deck for the hounds to fetch. The duo had been a real pain in my ass before Jenni's rescue mission. They hadn't quite warmed up to me, but at least they had backed off with the pranks and smart-mouthing.

I hadn't realized until recently that they were a couple. Alex and Kate were mostly quiet about their private life, but

I'd seen the aftermath of one of their love spats play out on the job a time or two. It was enough to cause concern, though they did manage to get their work done on time.

Their relationship was probably something I was supposed to report to Grim. I just couldn't bring myself to stir the pot. After all, the thing had just settled. Besides, Grim hadn't minded putting Kevin and Josie on the same team.

Kate tossed her head back to sweep her bangs out of her eyes. She caught sight of me and gave a short nod in greeting. Alex followed her line of sight and did the same. It felt good to have reapers treating me with respect, even if it wasn't full-blown admiration. I'd spent more than my fair share of time being the black sheep of Reapers Inc.

Arden Faraji's nod was more genuine, but that might have been because it was all I got from him most mornings. He spoke so little, he was often mistaken for mute. Everyone had tried their luck with him at one point or another. He had the rare ability to humiliate a person by not saying a single word. I wasn't even sure he knew when he was doing it. His height and dark complexion were intimidating enough, but add in the predatory silence, and he was downright scary sometimes. Today, Josie was testing the waters, trying to talk shop with him while she restrung her bow.

Kevin and I made a grand total of six. We were a modest unit, and to be honest, we could have used a few more reapers. The workload was heavy lately, due to wars and malnutrition in the mortal realm. The Mother Goose Unit was experiencing a spike in souls, too. Of course, with disappearing reapers, no one was brave enough to request extra hands, least of all me. I was the youngest unit captain and the highest on Grim's shit list. I wouldn't be giving him a reason to question my competency any time soon.

Josie finished with her bow and huffed out a defeated sigh in Arden's direction before turning to me. "Lay it on us, boss lady." It was only half sarcasm, and I could appreciate that.

Josie was by far the superior reaper. She had probably taken more classes at the academy than everyone on the team put together. Her resentment of my sudden string of promotions had faded off after I'd let her in on some of the baggage and blackmail that came with the fancy new title.

When I had everyone's attention, I handed out the soul dockets already filled in. Most days, I would have been more flexible, letting them divide a few harvests among themselves, but I was starting to get a feel for their strengths and preferences. I was also trying to save time, seeing as how our workload had grown. Luckily, no one balked. Not even Josie, who usually had two cents to throw in any time I took Kevin with me for the day. I let her take the hounds.

It was no secret that Grim had dumped Kevin on me as some sort of misplaced retribution after the death of his last second-in-command, Coreen Bendura. He had even paid the tuition for my mentoring class since I hadn't been certified to have an apprentice. It didn't seem to cross his mind that Kevin was the one suffering the most from the arrangement. Josie had taken the brunt of the responsibilities once she and Kevin hit it off, but Grim wouldn't officially transfer him under her supervision for that very reason.

I wasn't completely useless as a mentor. Hey, at least I was certified now. I was also the only mentor who was simultaneously captain of a specialty unit. I liked to think that fact added to Kevin's prestige as a reaper, but the truth was, most mentoring reapers did freelance work because it allowed for more quality one-on-one time with their apprentices. That's what I was aiming for today.

Part of my agenda was due to Jack's revelation. Kevin had applied for the demon defense course. It made me feel as if I weren't doing my job as a mentor. If he took the class, it would look like I wasn't trained well enough to pass the knowledge onto my own apprentice. The new semester at the academy kicked off Monday. I didn't have much time to convince Kevin to drop the class, but I was going to give it my best.

After everyone else had coined off to their first harvests, Kevin and I headed to L.A., where a police chase was about to lead to an eight-car pileup, a shootout followed by an explosion, and seventeen deaths.

I hadn't put anything too strenuous on our docket, and I spaced things out so we would have plenty of time to small talk in between stops. I wanted to ease into the conversation, but I wasn't very good at these things, and Kevin was no idiot. I wasn't sure if it was my interest in his attempts at Latin this morning or my sudden desire for mentor-apprentice time that tipped him off, but he was the one to break the ice while we watched the clock from a café near the projected crash site.

"I guess Beelzebub told you I applied for the demon defense course?" He blew across the top of his steaming

Phantom Café to-go cup and took a sip. We could enjoy the mortal café setting, but the humans couldn't see or hear us, so it was BYOC, *bring your own coffee.*

I swirled the contents of my own cup and tried not to look as offended as I felt. "Why didn't you tell me?" If he was going to cut right to it, there was no reason I shouldn't, too.

"Let's face it, Lana. You've been really busy since you made captain, and I know you didn't particularly enjoy the demon defense training course." He blushed and looked away. "Well, the actual learning parts of it anyway."

I followed his blush with one of my own. The fact that Bub and I were an item had painted lusty scenes in everyone's mind. Not that there hadn't been plenty of lusty scenes, but there had definitely been some learning going on, too.

"You're right." I cleared my throat. "The *learning* parts of the training course were not fun, but I did, in fact, learn. I had planned to train you myself. Why would you waste tuition on a class you could essentially get for free?"

Kevin rolled his eyes and gave me half a grin. "You mean being busy and hating learning isn't reason enough for me to look elsewhere?"

"I don't hate learning."

Kevin snorted.

"Okay. I hate learning. But that doesn't mean that I wasn't planning to teach you everything Bub will teach you in his class."

Kevin sipped his coffee. "I think it will be easier on both of us this way. Josie's even thinking about taking the class next semester."

"Really?"

Something about the Lord of the Flies assigning my crew homework was just too weird. I began to say something more, but it was cut short as sirens erupted outside. The crash was right on schedule.

"Coffee break's over."

Kevin and I exited the café and slipped in behind the forming crowd, opting to lean against the building rather than over the curb like the humans on hand. A few seconds later, a scene any newscaster would have traded their soul for played out before us. Pedestrians screamed. Tires squealed. Metal crunched. There were no fancy action movie stunts. Just a moron under the influence of something a bit shadier than video games and heavy metal, tearing through a crowded street in a retro death machine.

The car finally came to a stop when it smashed into the concrete wall of a parking garage. Said moron crawled out of a broken window and began firing at the squad of police cars surrounding him. He was a tall, lanky fellow in overalls and a stained tee shirt. One arm flopped uselessly at his side, bones poking through in a few places. His eyes were big, black saucers, and his gaping mouth showed more gums than teeth as he bellowed out a phlegmy howl of laughter. Yup. Definitely under the influence. I wasn't sure what kind of attitude we'd get from his soul, but I was already picturing him chained up down in the spare room off the hold.

Kevin flinched as the officers shot the man down. Twenty bullets to do the job of one. It was severe overkill, and some shameless family member would be sure to sue the department for it, but if the look in that crazy bastard's eyes weren't enough to make someone pull the trigger, nothing was.

"You want the belle of the ball, or should I take him?" I glanced over at Kevin and crinkled my nose.

He swallowed. "Go ahead. I'll backtrack and grab the few that didn't make it to the finale."

"Fair enough." I headed off to collect the catch of the day.

Black smoke billowed through the shredded hood of the getaway car, and the engine clicked and hissed out an ominous warning. I picked up my stride, wanting to avoid the impending explosion mentioned on the harvest docket.

Mr. Overdose Overalls was surprisingly calm, once I relieved him of his doped-up body. He even made a friend in the time he spent down in the hold since we didn't have to chain him up after all. It was almost a shame that he was Hell bound. *Almost.* Drugs can really put a kink in a person's fate. The friend he made was obviously not from the batch of souls we collected from the guy's inglorious last stand.

I didn't want to push Kevin too much, especially seeing as how he was onto me, so I bided my time. We waded through the day, collecting a plane crash here, and an apartment fire there. When we arrived at the ship with our last load of souls, there was half an hour to spare before Josie was due back. Just as I had planned.

"Wanna try out that Latin again?" I asked after we'd closed up the hatch on the main deck.

Kevin shrugged. "Sure. I could use a head start in Beelzebub's class."

"Seriously? You're really going to take it?" I popped a fist on my hip and glared at him.

"What's the big deal?" Kevin shrugged again as red splotches stained his cheeks.

"My reputation is fragile right now, okay? I'd just like to go a whole month without a new rumor sprouting."

We circled the hatch and stopped by the captain's cabin to strip off our robes before heading upstairs. The poop deck was the highest level on the ship. It was above the quarterdeck, where the helm and navigation room were located. It was also the worst possible place to play with fire. Not so much while we were docked, but being on the far aft side of the ship, it would be a serious hazard once we set sail.

"Why exactly did you bring Pinocchio up here?" My crummy mood injected more disdain into the question than I intended, and Kevin flinched.

"It's less visible from the main deck, and I didn't want an audience. Kate and Alex aren't exactly cheerleaders when it comes to these things." He squinted at the dummy's chest and poked at a charred spot that might have been from this morning's small victory.

"You can say that again. Still, if you're going to practice while we're sailing, be sure to move to the forecastle deck. If you set my sails on fire, you're not going to like your soul docket for a good long while."

Kevin nodded and positioned himself halfway across the deck. He waited for my cue before aiming his palm at the dummy again.

"*Sanctus Incendia*," he said correctly but without the proper inflection. Nothing happened.

I sighed. "That's great if you're trying to give the thing heartburn."

Kevin rolled his eyes but quickly cleared his throat before trying again, a bit louder this time. The result was a repeat of the morning smoke and sparks act.

I pursed my lips and thought a moment. "I've seen you in battle, Kevin. You're never that calm. Can you seriously tell me that's how you'd address a demon trying to eat your face off? You've seen me do the incantation before. That kind of force isn't for show. It's a necessary energy you have to put behind the words if you really mean them."

Kevin huffed, and his cheeks fired up again. He thrust his palm out once more. "*Sanctus Incendia!*" he growled.

There was less smoke this time. The fire sparked to life inches from his hand and shot true, sending poor Pinocchio up in flames. Kevin's jaw dropped as he turned back to me.

"Good!" I clapped my approval. "Now, where's the fire extinguisher?"

"Uh?" He scratched his head. "We have a fire extinguisher?"

My clapping stopped dead. "You're practicing fire incantations on my ship without a fire extinguisher?"

Kevin held up his hands, clenching and unclenching his fingers in a helpless frenzy. "I didn't expect it to actually work. It hasn't until now. Shit!"

The dummy was now engulfed in flames. Kevin looked around desperately, and then he made a flying leap at the thing, kicking it off the deck and into the sea.

I blinked stiffly and shook my head before walking over to look past the railing. "You owe me a new dummy. And a fire extinguisher for being stupid."

Kevin's ears burned bright red. "Yeah, sorry 'bout that."

"What'd I miss?" Josie coughed as she came up the stairs, fanning her hand in front of her face. "Smells like burnt toast up here."

"Your boyfriend nearly set our ship on fire." I raised an annoyed brow at him.

"You got the incantation to work?" Josie said with a grin, completely ignoring my accusation.

"Thanks to me." I folded my arms and stuck out my hip. "Guess he doesn't need that demon defense course after all."

"Grief, Lana." Josie huffed and rolled her eyes in time with Kevin. "I thought you'd be relieved to get out of extra training duty. I mean, I know how much you were looking forward to giving up your evenings and weekends to hit the books with Kevin—"

"You think I won't?" I glared at her, but there wasn't much malice in the look. She was right. I wasn't looking forward to it—but I *was* planning to do it.

Josie held out a hand. "If you're worried about looking bad, why don't you write Kevin a recommendation so it looks like it was your idea? Lots of apprentices take additional classes.”

“Shit.” I slapped a hand over my forehead. “I promised Clair Kramer that I would put in a good word with Bub.”

Josie’s eyebrows shot up. “Grace Adaline’s apprentice asked *you* to vouch for him?” She really knew how to sucker punch me in the ego sometimes.

“Why wouldn’t he? I’m a unit captain. He’s of the same generation as my apprentice. I’m the only person who’s taken the course so far.”

Josie’s nose curled up. “And the instructor is your boyfriend.”

“See if I write *you* a recommendation.” I tilted my chin in the air.

She shook her head. “We should really set sail if we want to beat rush-hour traffic.”

“Let me grab my bag from the cabin.”

“I thought you were coming with us,” Kevin said.

“Yeah, when I thought we were going to be working on your Latin. Can’t exactly do that without a practice dummy or a fire extinguisher. Besides, I have a couple of recommendation letters to write now anyway.”

“Yes!” Kevin high-fived Josie.

If they wanted to consider it a victory over my authority, so be it. I guess I could count it as a win, too. No extra apprentice lessons meant more wine and boat sex with Bub. You wouldn’t catch me complaining about that.

CHAPTER FOUR

*"War is eternity jammed into frantic minutes that will fill a life-
time with dreams and nightmares."*
—*John Cory*

My plan to avoid Grim was shot to hell, not only by Kevin and Josie's gloating atmosphere that had ejected me from the ship but also by the fact that Grim was lurking in my office when I returned to Reapers Inc. In the chair behind my desk, to be exact, peering at me over five remaining buckets of daisies.

The light filtering in through my window was fading as dusk pulled down the sky. It threw gloomy shades of yellow and orange over the stark angles of Grim's face and his perfectly tailored navy suit. His skin looked almost transparent next to the rich material. It turned his eyes into black holes that tried to suck all the life from the room.

He grunted at my surprise and folded his hands over a stack of manila envelopes and back issues of *Limbo Weekly* scattered across my desk. His eyes drifted from the daisies to the empty walls and then back to me.

"As much as I'm paying you, you would think you could afford a quality decorator." He stayed in my chair, but the image of him working Loki over with a serrated knife and a pair of pliers held my tongue in place.

I dropped my duffle bag on one of the guest chairs and sat in the other, slowly knotting my hands in my lap. "I'll make an appointment with one next week."

Grim's brow dropped into an exasperated line. My politeness clearly irritated him as much as my defiance had before.

"Amazingly enough, I'm not here to discuss your pathetic décor."

"Okay." I didn't point out that he was the one who had brought it up.

Grim smoothed his tie and picked up a sealed file lying on my desk. "Ms. Fang tells me that she's briefed you on tomorrow's mission." I nodded. "I couldn't grant her pardon for the others. Your unit is already overbooked. Which is the second reason I'm here." He tossed the file across the desk.

At first, I had thought it was Jenni's mission, but it was awfully dense for details on one assignment.

"Recruit pool?" I read from the label on the corner of the file.

"Congratulations, Harvey. I'm entrusting you to hand select two new reapers for your unit. Ms. Fang seems to think you're special mission material, and if she decides to pull you from fieldwork in the future, I expect your team to carry the burden. I can't very well rely on four reapers and your apprentice to get the job done, now can I?"

It was hard not to feel a pinch flattered, like Grim thought it would take *two* reapers to cover my workload. "Thank you, sir."

He rolled his eyes and flicked his hand at me. "Oh, please. I just don't have the time to pick them out myself. Don't bother with it tonight. You've got a mission to go over." He scooped up another file and tossed it toward me. "Turn in some names by Monday. If you live that long."

I looked up from the mission file and swallowed. "I did suggest sending the Nephilim Guard after Caim instead."

"As did I." Grim groaned and stood up from my desk. "Try not to let my new second-in-command get herself killed. It's bad for morale and even worse for business."

I was rendered speechless long enough for him to stalk out of my office. Grim was a cold bastard, but that had been a little much, even coming from him. Dirtying his hands after so many centuries had changed him. Something told me that if Jenni and I didn't return from this mission, the only emotion he'd register would be annoyance at the inconvenience it would cause him. It made me nervous, for my sake and Jenni's.

I waited for my heart to drop out of my throat before collecting the files and leaving. The lights down the hall and in the lobby had been turned off, and Ellen had gone home for the day. The office color scheme had drained to a dusty yellow, courtesy of the evening light creeping in through the wall of windows that circled Grim's fortress. Thankfully, I didn't run into anyone on my way through the main lobby on the first floor.

I took the travel booths straight home and was glad to find the condo empty. I needed to quiet my mind before taking a look at the mission file. It had been eating at my thoughts all day. Another potentially lethal secret to keep the others company. It was getting crowded in my skeleton closet.

I calmed my nerves with a hot shower before lighting a lavender oil lamp Gabriel had bought for me on his last trip to Heaven. Then I double-checked the condo and locked my bedroom door. In yoga pants and with wet hair, I dumped the contents of the mission file out onto my bed and shuffled the pieces around until they began to make sense.

There were ship blueprints and rebel profiles mixed in with anonymous tip-off reports. A schedule detailed every minute of our morning. Jenni had planned the mission out like a single mother planned a trip to Disneyland for six. And I thought Josie was anal. Jenni had even included a sticky note reminding me not to drink too much coffee since bathroom breaks would interrupt the flow of things. At least she'd kept the schedule tight enough that we would be finished by lunch. That is if everything went according to plan and we didn't die first.

Up close, with a zillion facts and diagrams laid out before me, the mission almost seemed plausible. But when I stepped back and really tried to process what we would be doing the next morning, Jenni kept coming up a few cups short of a tea party. This was madness. Even if I had a week to go over everything, there was no way I could remember the contents of that file. It was too much information with not enough time to absorb. The problem was, by the time it really did sink in, the intel would be stale.

The front door slammed.

"Lana, you home?" Josie shouted from the kitchen.

"Coming." I shuffled together all the bits of the mission and stuffed them back into the file before grabbing the recruits folder and going out to meet Josie and the hounds.

Saul mowed me over the second I came out of my room, knocking me to the floor. His wet snout burrowed in behind my ear as he whimpered out his excited greeting. Then he lapped up the side of my face before bounding past me and up onto my bed.

Coreen, who was entirely too sophisticated to be a hellhound, nudged her head under my hand as she passed, letting her body brush between my arm and ribcage. It was her subtle, sneaky way of getting in a pet without looking too desperate for attention. Sometimes, I could swear she was a cat in a past life. She gave me a quick sniff and leapt up to join Saul on my bed.

Josie was alone in the kitchen when I finally picked myself up and rounded the corner. She unpacked a noisy bag full of Chinese takeout.

I pulled out a barstool and sat at the breakfast bar, discarding the recruits file on the counter and helping myself to a container of coconut chicken. "Where's Kevin?"

A pout tugged down the corners of Josie's mouth as she handed me a pair of chopsticks. "Working on the ship. He should be finishing up on that back cabin soon. He spends all of his free time there lately."

I shrugged. "It'll be nice having your own cabin. I know I won't miss interrogating you every time I spot a questionable stain on my bunk sheets."

"I won't miss that either. Grief. It's not like you use that bed anyway."

"Not anymore, I don't."

Josie rolled her eyes and popped open a container of eg-grolls. She forked a couple onto a plate, adding a heap of fried rice and a scoop of cashew chicken. There were half a dozen unopened containers lined up along the counter.

"What's with the smorgasbord?" I asked, cracking open the chopsticks.

"I couldn't decide. Plus, I knew you'd probably invite yourself to dinner. I guess I'm just in a nice mood today. Or maybe I didn't feel like eating alone again." She laughed dryly. "Three roommates, and they've all gone recluse on me."

The coconut chicken became hard to swallow. I'd gone all day without even thinking about letting the demons out of the bag, and then Josie had to go and finger my guilt button.

I wanted to tell her about the mission. Hell, I wanted her to go on the mission with us. But Grim was right. I couldn't afford for half my team to take the day off tomorrow. Plus, we lived with Jenni. She and Josie had been roommates before we all moved in together. I wasn't about to take the chance that Jenni knew Josie well enough to notice when she was hid-ing something.

I hesitated too long, lost in thought and rolling around bad ideas. My silence always spoke louder than I intended. Josie paused to glare at me, in that way that usually meant she knew I was holding out on her, but they would serve ice cream in Hell before she'd beg for details. My guilt instantly mor-phed into panic, but thankfully, Josie beat me to fill the void.

"What's that?" she asked, nodding at the recruits file on the counter.

Finally, something I *could* talk to her about. "Grim's letting me select two new recruits for the unit."

"Really?" And just like that, Josie changed gears. Her face lit up as she reached for the folder, mindfully ignoring the elephant in the room.

"Yeah. You wanna pick them out?"

Her mouth dropped into a tiny *o*. "Are you sure?"

"Yeah." Goodbye guilt. "I'm kinda overloaded with paperwork right now anyway."

Josie opened the folder and flipped through the first few pages, careful not to dribble duck sauce on them. "We need someone young and eager to please, but with at least a little more experience than low-risk harvesting. Unless they have an impressive academy transcript. We could make an exception for that."

"You wanna take the weekend to go over the candidates? I have to turn in some names by Monday. Let's get together Sunday night to go over your decision."

"Sure, okay." She nodded, more to herself than me, as she fingered through the resumes.

The silence was a comfortable one, and I was glad to have relieved Josie of her accusing, sourpuss pout. I hung around long enough to finish the coconut chicken. My stomach wasn't up for much more. By the time I made it back to my bedroom, I wished I had skipped dinner altogether. My nerves were slowly vibrating to earthquake proportions, making my stomach churn like a concrete mixer. Tomorrow's chance of survival was significantly lower than usual.

Never mind that Jenni had choreographed the mission out impeccably, even on such short notice. But the looming promise of death was enough to make the best-laid plans look like a botched game of red rover, and I didn't want to be the kid who assumed everyone would follow the rules, only to get clotheslined by some greasy-knuckled punk. Or have my face eaten off by a hellcat, which was unfortunately much more likely.

I paced across my room and rubbed away the chill growing up my arms. I needed to pull myself together long enough to get a good night's sleep. I needed a distraction.

Bub had recently bought me a tablet. I fetched it out of my nightstand drawer and logged online via Holly House's wireless network. It was Thursday night, but something told me that Bub would wait until the very last second to turn in his class roster to the academy dean. I shot Jack a quick email, requesting that Kevin and Clair make the final cut. Then I rummaged around in my closet for a while, looking for something to wear on my Friday night date with Bub, if I lived to see it. Picking out an outfit was a small confidence boost. It was an illusion of hope. Like I really thought I might prevail. And it was the only mood lifter I had readily available, so I took it.

I went to bed early, snuggling in under the covers and tucking my feet beneath the mountain of fearsome adorable snoring at the end of my bed. The hounds were enough to chase the nightmares away for now. Besides, I'd have real-life horrors to deal with by morning. Knowing that would help me flip the bird at any villains who managed to slip into my dreams.

Somewhere between too damn late and too damn early, a whimper cut through my dreamless sleep. The hounds didn't usually rouse me for breakfast until at least six. After Saul had nudged his wet nose under my arm, I realized the noise wasn't coming from my room. It was coming from down the hall. The villains I'd dismissed were plotting in someone else's nightmares.

I slipped on my bathrobe and tiptoed out into the darkness. The hardwood floor was cold on my bare feet, and it sent a chill through me. A thin light spilled out of Jenni's room. No one had said anything when she started leaving her door ajar after her week with the rebels.

Even with the Latin protection prayers running along the trim of our heavy duty front door, I found myself holding my breath at times, listening for the sound of death coming for me. Not Grim. Not yet anyway. But after Loki had managed to slip past the Holly House defenses, I wasn't as sure of my safety as I'd once been.

Holly said that since Loki intended to spy and not harm us on the premises, he'd been able to slip through some loophole in the wards. I just didn't want my neck getting stuck in that loophole.

Jenni's concerns had to be worse than mine. The whimpering boiled over into a full-on sob as I reached her door. I lifted my hand, stopping just shy of knocking.

"Jenni?" I whispered, easing the door open.

She lay curled on her side facing away from me. The bed-side lamp cast a blue light over the room. It stretched over her back, tickling the edges of her face and shoulder. Darkness pooled in the shadow she made on the other side of the bed.

"Jenni?" I tried again.

She froze, and I was sure she'd awakened, but then another sob slipped from her. "I don't know. I don't know. I don't know," she mumbled over and over, growing louder each time. Josie and Kevin would wake soon—if they hadn't already.

I had the good sense to click on her bedroom light before approaching her. As my vision refocused, I circled the bed. Jenni's eyes were squeezed shut so tightly that her entire face was creased. Tears dripped from her lashes as her fists tangled in the sheets, stretching the fabric to the point of tearing.

"Jenni?" I said louder this time, giving her shoulder a quick shake before jumping back.

She yelped and rasped in a sharp breath as she woke, her eyes shooting open like I'd just resuscitated her with jumper cables.

"Am I late? Did I miss my alarm?" She blinked and sat up suddenly, rubbing both hands over her face roughly.

"No. You were just having too much fun in your sleep for me to tolerate it any longer." I yawned and tucked my hands into the pockets of my robe.

"Oh." Her face soured as she caught my meaning, and she looked down at her lap. "Did I wake anyone else?"

"I think I got to you in time. Though I am really curious about what it is that you don't know." I slumped down onto the bed next to her, now that I was sure she was awake and not going to mistake me for an intruder. Getting stabbed in the face with the knife she probably kept under her pillow was not how I wanted to start the day.

Jenni rolled her shoulders, trying to hide her trembling. "Well, clearly I don't know." She stared off into space. "I probably would have told him after the second day if I had actually known anything."

It was my turn to tremble. If the rebels had taken me instead of Jenni, I wondered how long I would have lasted before spilling my guts. Aside from despising me, Grim clearly had other reasons for not wanting me as his second-in-command.

Jenni shifted awkwardly next to me. This was the first time I had actually been in her room. My tired eyes roved over her personal space with vague interest. Her décor paused somewhere between cliché and extraordinary.

Three enormous scrolls stretched down the wall opposite her bed, filled with breathtaking scenes painted in traditional Japanese style. Cherry blossoms towered over geishas, and samurai warriors fought dragons atop jagged mountains. Two oversized fans were anchored to the wall behind her bed, detailed with more cherry blossoms and Japanese calligraphy. An antique tea set and table were displayed in the far corner of the room, and a dainty vanity sat along the wall between the bedroom and bathroom doors.

I yawned and stretched my neck. "If I add booze to my coffee, are you gonna rat me out to Grim?"

That earned a soft laugh. "I won't, as long as you add some to mine, too."

"Deal."

Jenni stood and stretched her arms over her head. Her thin tee shirt rose up over her stomach and lower back, exposing a web of fresh scars. "I'm going to grab a quick shower."

"I'll save mine for after the spiked coffee."

The hounds had resumed their snoozing, I realized as I stepped back out into the hallway. Their snores were joined by another set coming from Josie and Kevin's room. For a second, I was envious. Even when I conked out early, I couldn't catch a full night of sleep. It was sad, really.

I shuffled into the kitchen and clicked on the dim light over the sink. Being awake this early was bad enough without blinding myself. I fired up the coffee pot and set out our favorite mugs. I'd found mine at one of the harbor market booths. It featured a cartoon reaper with a sexy leg and high heel popping out of a slit in her robe. *Death, be a lady tonight* was scrawled out beneath her in curly letters.

Jenni's favorite mug was black with white block letters. It read *Confucius say, man who fart in church sit in own pew*. It was the only favorite thing I knew about her. Our roomie-bonding time was limited to the barely conscious hours of the morning when we shared a cup or three of coffee in blissful silence. It was like we were socializing in our sleep. There wasn't time for much else, but it seemed to be working out okay so far.

I laid my head on the cool counter, letting the steady drip of the coffeepot lull me into a meditative state. The picture window in the living room was dark, punctuated by only a few distant streetlights, stretching down Memorial Drive. As the first hint of dawn broke the horizon, the farthest streetlight went out. A shiver tiptoed down my spine as I remembered the suffocating doom spell that served as the rebel fury Tisiphone's calling card. Tisiphone was dead. *I killed her*, I reminded myself. The thought steadied me, keeping the panic of the day's agenda at bay.

Jenni entered the kitchen, breaking my trance right as the coffeepot chimed. I stood, but she waved me back down. "I'll get it."

She took her coffee black, like Josie, but I liked mine with all the bells and whistles. Jenni didn't quite have the alchemy down yet, but she was getting close. At this hour, I could hardly think, let alone complain. I watched her mix in sugar, creamer, and a healthy shot of Irish whiskey. She paused over her mug and pressed her lips together before compromising and pouring in half a shot.

"What'd you think of the mission file? Find any kinks in the plan?" she asked, handing over my mug.

"It's, um, detailed." I nodded my head slowly and took a long drink. "There's not a lot of room for error."

"Oh?" Jenni frowned.

"What if something goes wrong midway through? Are we improvising? Is there a plan B that I missed? Or are we going to abandon ship if one of the puzzle pieces doesn't fit quite right?"

"The pieces will fit. Trust me." Jenni chugged down her coffee and filled a second cup, minus the whiskey, before sitting down next to me. She was quiet for a long while, her eyes unblinking and her forehead creased by some mixture of worry and determination.

"The pieces have to fit," she said, turning to look at me. "I can't live like this anymore, always looking over my shoulder. He has to die, and he has to do it today. I won't fail. I can't fail." Panic bubbled up in her voice and her eyes glazed over.

"Okay," I said softly.

The guilt I felt over questioning her careful planning was overshadowed by a ripening fear that tightened around my insides like an icy fist. I could at least agree with her about one thing. The pieces had to fit. If they didn't, then this really would turn out to be a suicide mission. The look in Jenni's eyes told me that she wouldn't be coming back if she couldn't bring Caim's head back with her.

Jenni put her mug down and straightened. "I have some business to attend to before we take off. I'll meet you at the dock after you finish with your unit meeting."

CHAPTER FIVE

"Courage is being scared to death...and saddling up anyway."
—John Wayne

After Jenni had left, panic set in. Six a.m. found me hunched over the toilet in my bathroom, dry-heaving long after my stomach had evicted more bile than any self-respecting stomach should ever contain. If I survived this, I was going to have my head examined. I was also going to avoid Jenni until she got *her* head back on straight. Her issues be damned. Screw her special missions. I didn't have a death wish.

I made a point to stay in the shower until I heard Josie and Kevin leave with the hounds. Then I threw on a pair of faded jeans and a tank top. Keeping my old boots had been a good call. They were already stained with demon blood, so at least I wouldn't be making any sacrifices to the fashion gods today.

I strapped my throwing stars around my thigh. Then I took a whetstone and some oil to my battle axe before slinging it over my shoulder. I usually saved my robe for after the morning meeting, but walking through the city dressed to kill would probably defeat the whole top-secret aspect of the mission. I tugged a robe over my head, tossed a few vials of holy water into my duffle bag along with a can of angelica mace, and made a hasty exit before I lost my nerve.

I kept the morning meeting short. The only person who seemed to notice my wardrobe shift was Josie, which was expected. She noticed everything. The only thing that saved me from interrogation was the fact that her soul docket was borderline impossible. Her eyes grew as they took in the list. She blinked up at me a few times and bit her bottom lip.

"You'll have Kevin and the hounds today," I said.

"I figured that much." She didn't say anything else in front of the unit, but I knew I'd be in for a chewing later.

All the dockets were heavy today to make up for my absence, so everyone left early to get a head start. I didn't want to linger on the ship too long, for fear Josie and Kevin would be back soon to stash souls in the hold. So, I left and ventured farther down the dock, closer to where Jenni was supposed to meet me and tried to stay out of everyone's way.

The main pier ran wide down the center, pointing out into the sea and branching into thinner walkways on both sides. At the end, the final boardwalk reached out farther than the others, forming a *T*. It spawned off more walkways that had been added on in the last century. Steamboats, ferries, yachts, and an assortment of other mismatched sailing vessels filled the boat slips, leaving only a few spots open to receive the occasional guest or tourist transport.

Not many reapers delivered souls directly by coin. The price of delivery was figured into our commission like per diem business meals. It was our call, but it was an easy one.

When asked to choose between a lobster dinner and a thousand dollars, PB&J doesn't sound half bad.

Morning light swelled at the edges of Limbo City's sunless sky. There was a damp coolness to the air, stirred up from the bowels of the sea as it sloshed against the rock wall lining the east coast of the city. Reapers randomly zapped out of sight as they coined off to start the day's harvesting. When the dock cleared, I spotted Jenni at the far south end of the outer pier, directing a small lot of souls into the sea. I hung back a few minutes and waited for her to finish.

Atheists, agnostics, and the generally non-religious went into the sea, where they sloshed around for a few decades until the Three Fates Factory sucked them up and shipped them back to the mortal realm. It seemed harmless enough but, sometimes, I wondered if it wasn't a fate worse than Hell.

Floating around in a sea of souls for years and years sounded so utterly boring and depressing. At least Hell was interesting, though when I bent the rules and got a soul out of walking the plank, I generally tried to get them into one of the heavens.

When I did do things by the book, convincing a soul to take that leap into the sea was never especially pleasant. All reapers have their own tactics for getting the job done. Some who are less blessed in the decency department have no problem making souls literally walk the plank. Some use the long reach of their scythe to nudge their charges off the pier. The newer reapers tend to spend more time soothing souls with inspirational tales of future lives to come. Some flat-out lie.

Just go for a little dip. You need to be nice and clean before I drop you off at Heaven's gate.

I opt for hard facts. It's honest, and it saves time. *This is my job. This is your fate. We'll meet again, at a much later date.* The poetry seems to calm them, too.

Whatever method is used, the outcome is the same. The sea opens its enchanting maw and swallows them down, where they cease to function as individuals. They become one with the gray currents and waves of deaf, mute ghosts waiting for their time to shine again. I wasn't particularly fond of the chore. I mean, it wasn't like we were drowning puppies or anything, but let's face it, it was depressing.

When Jenni's last soul took the plunge, she turned and waved me over. I glanced around the harbor as I approached. The only craft waiting at the far end of the pier was an antiquated Chinese dragon boat, which was basically a canoe that seated twenty. My heart steadily plummeted as I envisioned us flipping ass over elbow while trying to battle demons on the sea. We were going to need some serious circus training if that was Jenni's vessel of choice.

My stomach soured with each step until I came to a stop in front of her. "Please, please, *please*, tell me you are joking."

Jenni blinked a few times and followed my line of sight to the little bath toy of a boat. Her face flushed. "You said you read the file. Tell me you read the file."

"Of course I read the file." I felt my face warm. "I read it *several* times."

"Then surely you didn't overlook the part about taking my primary transport."

"No, I read that part." I rubbed a hand over my forehead. "I just wasn't aware that your primary transport was a canoe."

"It's not." A grin tugged at her mouth. "I thought Josie would have told you. I guess I assume too much." Her hand pointed out to the empty space next to the dragon boat. "That's my primary transport."

My eyebrows shot up. "It's invisible?"

"Sort of." She laughed. "It's a research submarine."

I peered out over the sea, really following the line of her arm this time, and sure enough, there was an escape trunk poking up out of the water about ten yards from the dock. It was made of some clear material, blending almost flawlessly into the soulish matter of the sea.

"Huh." I tilted my head. The mission suddenly didn't seem entirely hopeless.

"Son of a virgin. You're joking, right?" A sharp wind rolled up my backside as Gabriel landed on the dock next to me, clad in a tattered work robe. His brows knit together as he squinted out to where Jenni pointed, clearly having overheard the tail end of our conversation. The submarine bobbed under the waves. Every so often, the water thinned enough to flash us a glimpse of what hid beneath.

"How much extra buoyancy do you suppose it will have with a passenger who can walk on water?" I grinned.

Gabriel groaned. "That's the big cheese's resume, pilgrim. Mine has more badassery and fewer pedicures."

I slugged him on the arm. "Don't look so green. I'm sure Jenni knows how to drive this beast."

Gabriel swallowed and tilted his head back. His blond curls tumbled away from his face as he pulled in a deep breath. "I knew I should have stayed in bed." Then he glanced back at me. "You're in an awfully good mood for someone who might die today."

"I'm relieved. Five minutes before you got here, I thought we were taking a canoe out to meet Caim."

"And that's somehow worse than a submarine?"

I smiled. Gabriel's presence was reassuring, as was his nervousness. It made my own nerves pale in comparison. Until Maalik arrived.

The Keeper of Hellfire arrived by coin, probably back from a meeting at the Inferno Chateau, where he occasionally convened with the Hell Committee. Maalik's arrival was subtle, though his outfit was anything but. He had already changed into his mission attire. The black leather pants, matching vest, and leather gauntlets were an intimidating ensemble. Add in the majestic silver wings, and it was also enough to make any warm-blooded girl swoon. Just because I couldn't handle him as an overbearing, pants-wearing boyfriend, did not mean that I was incapable of appreciating how his butt looked in said pants.

Maalik gave me a measured look and a nod. The sourness of our breakup had mostly dissolved since our last encounter. I knew he still cared about me, and he knew that we were not getting back together. It was an effort, on both sides, to accept this as neutral information, instead of a reason to feel scorn.

Maalik reached out to slap Gabriel on the back. "Good to see you again, friend."

"Likewise." Gabriel returned the gesture with a genuine smile.

It was strange to see them so agreeable with each other, especially since Gabriel had loathed Maalik when I first started dating him. Now that they were both heavily involved in Eternity politics, the two angels were spending more and more leisure time together. I didn't know how to feel about it, and I wasn't sure I had any right to feel anything at all. Though I was a little chagrined that Gabriel hadn't warmed up to Bub.

"All right." Jenni looked down at her watch. "We're right on schedule. Time to set this plan into motion."

She pulled a sheet of cardboard out of the floor of the dragon boat and threw it to me. I unfolded it and stepped in behind Maalik, lifting the cardboard up to backdrop his outspread wings.

Gabriel's nose crinkled as Jenni shook a can of black acrylic spray paint. "It's a good thing I have one of those fancy showers at Holly House to clean up in."

Jenni gave him a level look. "My botched paint job should be the least of your worries today."

Maalik held his breath as Jenni coated his wings. Since we were at the far end of the dock this late in the morning, the only witnesses we had to concern ourselves with were the pair of nephilim guards at the entrance. The assortment of reaper vessels made for good cover, though. Besides, the nephilim guards would never leave their assigned posts.

Jenni was precise with the paint, and only a faint mist escaped around Maalik's edges. What little I missed with the cardboard shot out past the dock and dissipated before reaching the sea. When Jenni finished with Maalik, I held the cardboard up behind Gabriel. It took two coats to darken his wings since they were a brilliant, glowing white. Jenni emptied the rest of the can in his hair and over his robe. She had been right about this being a botch job, but it didn't need to be perfect for what we were trying to pull off.

"This is going to really stink in such a confined space." Gabriel's voice took on a grating note. "Are you sure we shouldn't fly and meet you there?"

Jenni folded her arms. "We can't risk the paint drying too quickly. It will peel and flake off. We also can't risk drawing that much attention for so long before we arrive. Besides, the sub has a very advanced air purification system. You'll be fine."

Maalik's face tightened at the mention of the submarine. He didn't look surprised, but he was far from delighted.

We all piled into the dragon boat, and Jenni rowed us the short distance to the submarine's trunk. She twisted the wheel to the hatch, and we quickly climbed down the ladder and into the belly of her vessel. Jenni dropped an anchor from the dragon boat to keep it in place for our return.

The inside of the sub was bigger than I expected, with enough room to hold at least twenty souls. Jenni was a high-risk harvester, so it was plenty of room for her. It would have never worked for someone on the Posy Unit, who was ex-pected to harvest hundreds of souls at a time.

The ladder dropped us between an oblong bubble of a viewing room and the more secluded navigation chamber at the back. Computers and cameras that had once been used for research were anchored to a ledge that circled the viewing room, though they were powered down and coated in a fine layer of dust.

I pressed my face to the viewing glass, peering out into the dusty blue void. A transparent hand slid across the surface, making me jump back into Gabriel. He caught my shoulders, spotted what had startled me, and shuddered.

Maalik stayed near the center of the room, hands clenched at his sides. "Let's get this over with," he said, shifting his gaze from side to side as if keeping an eye on the sub would prevent it from imploding.

Jenni took us in with amused disbelief. "I've done this before, guys. You can relax. There's soda in the mini-fridge." She pointed toward the front of the observation room before disappearing into the navigation chamber.

An engine fired up, and we began to move. Gabriel hadn't let go of me, and his fingers only gripped my shoulders tighter as we lost buoyancy and sank into darker waters. The souls of the sea were more defined farther down, white outlines contrasting against the blue-black water. I never caught sight of a complete form, only a hand here and a face there. The bodies were layered upon each other in an indistinguishable pile of limbs. An occasional eye blinked at me, pondering my existence as much as I pondered its own.

After Jenni had set our coordinates, she joined us in the viewing room, where she had another laugh at our expense. "We're only about a hundred meters below the surface. Just deep enough to not be spotted."

"But it's so dark," Gabriel complained.

"Light only penetrates so far." Jenni walked past us to the mini-fridge and grabbed a soda. "We should be in position within fifteen minutes. Then I'll send up the periscope to watch for our target."

I pried Gabriel's fingers off my shoulders and decided to brave crossing the viewing room for a beverage. If anything was going to kill me today, chances were, a swarm of demons would be more likely.

I found a root beer at the back of the refrigerator and clinked cans with Jenni before cracking it open. "So, how is it your contact knows right where Caim's ship will be? That seems a little too accurate for a spot out in the middle of nowhere."

Jenni pressed her lips together. "We haven't figured out the method they're currently using to hide their base, but we've had several reports of rebel ships suddenly appearing on the sea. No harbor officials have reported them entering or exiting any of the afterlife ports. We've surveyed the entire sea—*twice*—to see if there is another island in use like the one we found last year. So far, we've turned up nothing."

She paused to take a drink of her soda and eyed Maalik. He was a council member and a staunch believer in the rules, but Jenni was, too. Maalik gave her a nod, assuring her that the details were sharable with Gabriel and me.

Jenni cleared her throat. "A pagan contact of mine managed to get a message out to Caim that he was interested in joining the rebel army. He was given coordinates for a meeting, which he passed along to me. In addition to killing Caim today, I also wouldn't mind discovering where the new rebel base is."

Gabriel paled. "You do realize that could mean the four of us against the entire rebel army, right? Have you lost your mind?"

Jenni was silent for a moment. She stared out at the souls beyond the viewing glass and finished her soda. "If everything goes according to plan, we'll be on and off Caim's ship in two minutes, tops. We'll strike like a snake and recoil beneath the sea before they even know what's happened."

The cold detachment in her voice settled into my stomach. My eyes met Gabriel's, and we exchanged worried looks.

The next fifteen minutes were agonizingly long. We all held our breath when Jenni launched the periscope, and true to schedule, announced that Caim's ship was in position only a moment later.

I shed my robe and tucked the angelica mace and holy water down inside my boots. The water around the submarine was brighter since we had migrated closer to the surface, but we were deep enough to go undetected for now. Souls moved more quickly beyond the viewing glass as if they could sense the tension building within the sub.

Jenni fastened a wide, leather belt around her waist and secured several sheathed blades at her hips. Then she dug a tin of war paint out of her bag and smeared her face with the black goop before passing it to me. I did the same. Though they were camouflaged, the angels were both going in bare-knuckled. Maalik's hands packed a fair amount of heat, being the Keeper of Hellfire and all. Gabriel was relying on sheer strength.

"I'll take Lana." Maalik stepped up beside me, only to be nudged back by Jenni.

"Like hell," she snapped. "We stick to the plan in the mission file. I didn't outline the specifics for negotiation." Her shoulders squared, and her chin lifted as she waited for Maalik to protest. He looked like he might until Gabriel rested a hand on his shoulder.

"I'll take good care of her," he said, placing his other hand on my shoulder.

"I'm right here, guys. And I wasn't included in this mission to play damsel in distress. Get over yourselves already." I pulled my shoulder away from Gabriel and picked up my battle axe before following Jenni to the ladder and through the hatch. The angels tailed us ruefully.

Once we reached sea level, we moved more quickly, trying not to draw attention to the submarine. Maalik slid past me and took Jenni into his arms. No sooner than they had taken flight, Gabriel scooped me up, and we followed suit.

Caim's ship hadn't changed much, except for the addition of a few dozen hellspawn scaling the masts and railings of the black boat. The main deck was an overflowing mass of leathery flesh and barbed tails. A herd of satyrs paraded around the quarterdeck, puffing into wooden panpipes, while sirens and succubi danced to the haunting tune, spinning frenzied circles around splintered mast poles. The wind ripped at their hair and grazed their naked bodies, leaving chapped patches along their thighs and breasts.

Caim lounged along the edge of the stern deck. His pale skin looked sickly and transparent. Despite the heat and the abundant nudity, he wore a thick, dark robe. His black wings were oily, almost sparkling in broad daylight. Where his chin and jawline ended, the flesh peeled away, leaving the length of his neck raw and tarry. The sight of him made me cringe. I couldn't imagine what it did to Jenni.

Caim reached out to fondle a siren as she spun by, clawing at her flesh with his blackened fingertips and leaving deep cuts that quickly welled with purple blood. He cackled, flashing sharp teeth and black gums. The siren hardly spared him a gasp before falling under the spell of the satyr pipes once again. She swayed and rubbed against a succubus, smearing the forgotten blood until they were both coated. A leathery-winged demon dipped down to steal a taste with his forked tongue.

Gabriel's grip under my arms tightened. "This is a terrible idea." He grunted under the weight of my axe and me. The paint on his wings probably wasn't helping either. One slid up my arm, and I hissed from the roughness of it.

"I agree, but it's a little late to turn back now." My heart accelerated in my chest as I scanned the ship, desperately searching for an opening. It was looking more and more like a crash landing would be our only option.

A few seconds later, Maalik rounded the stern with Jenni in tow. It had been a smart move putting me with Gabriel. Maalik would have never dropped me on Caim's ship, and the plan would have been shot all to hell. He glanced across the chaos to find Gabriel and me, and I could tell that I was still getting top billing on his worry list. I could live with that today I decided, taking in the scene unfolding beneath us.

Gabriel sucked in a tight breath. "Showtime." Then he dropped me on a pile of napping hellcats on the forecastle deck.

The move was both incredibly stupid and incredibly smart. I cursed him under my breath anyway as I brought my axe down on the neck of one of the beasts. The hellcats were fast, and they could fly. They would be the first to give chase when we fled, and they would be the most likely to catch us before we made it back to the submarine.

I pulled my axe from the first cat and sank it into the next. The creature gurgled out its defeat as my blade slid free, making a soggy sucking noise. I switched hands, using the opposite side of the double-headed axe to quicken the slaughter. The cats were the size of Clydesdales, so my advantage wouldn't last forever.

A demon clawed its way onto the forecastle deck and screeched out a battle cry, or what I assumed was a battle cry. It sounded more like a pterodactyl trying to mate with a bullfrog. It had six spidery arms to make up for its lack of legs, and each one ended in a skeletal hand tipped with jagged nails that oozed vicious, green fluid. It launched itself at me, but Gabriel swooped down and caught it, twisting two of the creature's arms behind its arched spine. He didn't waste time wrestling the thing, just pitched it over the deck railing before facing off with a bucking satyr.

I turned back to the litter of hellcats. I'd slain all but two. Unfortunately, they were now roused enough to fight back.

The first opened its jaws and howled at me, a long, deafening sound that made the pressure in my head swell, and my ears bleed. I was suddenly dizzy. I pressed my back to the foremast in the center of the deck. My axe felt heavier, and my knuckles popped as I tightened my grip. I was splattered with hellcat blood. It burned my skin and made the deck slippery.

My ears felt like they had cotton balls stuffed into them, but I heard Gabriel's warning in time to dodge a blow from the second cat. I lost my footing and landed hard on my side. The first beast pounced, but I rolled away, escaping with only a shallow swipe of claws that ripped through my tank top and grazed my ribcage.

I swung my axe behind me as I stood, taking out the cat's back two legs. The thing looked over its shoulder and hissed at me as the second fiend struck, slamming me to the deck floor. Its claws pressed down on my chest, stealing my breath, while its mangled maw of fangs snapped at my throat. I pressed the handle of my axe into its mouth, straining to keep it at bay. My head dangled over the edge of the deck, and I spotted a naked siren. She blinked curiously as she approached, completely oblivious to the creature trying to rip out my throat.

When her breasts were pressed against my forehead, she stopped and twirled a finger in my hair. "I know you," she cooed. "But where's your tender companion? The one I sang for." She giggled sweetly while the veins in my neck and forehead bulged and boiled beneath my flesh.

I wedged a leg under the hellcat and flipped the beast over the deck and at the siren. She squealed and ducked, taking a handful of my hair with her. My breath rushed back to me in a wave of euphoria. That had been too close. I gasped and rolled onto my stomach, pushing myself off the floor with trembling arms. The ship pitched, tossing me back down on the weathered boards. I groaned and lifted my head enough to glance back at the stern deck.

Strings of blood webbed across Jenni's face and arms as she wielded a katana blade through the herd of naked demons ambling about the quarterdeck. They had been expecting a new recruit, not an ambush. The battle was lost on many of them, swallowed by the chaos of their debaucherous party. Even Caim looked confused until Jenni sliced through the last siren standing between them.

There was no victory in her eyes when she plunged her blade through Caim's chest. She met him, nose-to-nose and unblinking, sinking her blade in all the way to the hilt. Caim's black eyes shuffled through pain, surprise, and panic as he saw through the war paint. Jenni waited for the recognition she deserved, and then she ripped the blade upward, splitting his torso and skull in half in one final stroke. Her vacant eyes found me, and she gave a quick nod before stepping up onto the outer railing and off the ship. Maalik caught her mid-air.

My vision spotted, and I realized I'd been holding my breath. A gurgling hiss sounded behind me. The hellcat I had amputated dragged itself toward me with its two front legs. Its wings were bent at an odd angle, but it managed to lift itself a few inches at a time, adding soggy thumps in between scratching the deck floor. I pulled myself upright and clutched my axe to my chest as Gabriel snatched me up from behind.

We left the leaderless hellions behind and fled for the submarine.

CHAPTER SIX

The claustrophobic atmosphere of the submarine was long forgotten, overpowered by an uneasy air of victory and relief. Maalik gave up his pretense and came to me right away, insisting that I let him clean and cover my mild wounds, though they were no worse than anyone else's.

"This bandage won't last, you realize." Gabriel sat in one of the swivel chairs by the viewing glass, wiping blood from his face with a towel.

"You think I need stitches?" I glanced down at the scratches on my ribcage, cringing when Maalik dabbed me with an alcohol wipe.

"No. I'm talking about this victory. It won't last." Gabriel shook his head. "We'll have a short stretch of peace, but then we'll be back in the dark, not knowing who the new rebel generals are."

Jenni refused to look at him. "I don't care who the new generals are, as long as they're not Caim."

She sat on the ledge that stretched around the viewing room and pulled her knees up to her chest. I had pictured victory more flattering on her, but at least the fake cheer she had been parading seemed to have faded for now.

Maalik finished dressing my wounds and slumped down in a chair beside Gabriel. "We're also not any closer to discovering the location of the rebel base."

Jenni pressed her face against the dark glass with a disheartened sigh. "I know."

"Hey!" I slapped Gabriel's arm. "I don't know about you all, but I kicked ass. This is one for the history books. We won and lived to fight another day. Don't look so grim."

That earned a few weak smiles, but the rest of the trip was spent in silent reflection. Gabriel and Maalik were right, of course. But Jenni deserved some semblance of peace, even if it had essentially morphed the big picture into a Picasso. We'd survived. It was enough for me.

When we reached the harbor, Gabriel invited Maalik back to Holly House to clean up. The nephilim guards gave us wary glances, but luckily, we didn't run into anyone else on the way home. We parted ways in the lobby of Holly House, and I didn't remember until Jenni and I reached our condo that I'd meant to ask Maalik about Winston. It could wait.

Jenni was gone when I emerged from the shower. Grim was not a patient man, and she would be eager to report our success. I didn't worry as much about the media frenzy that would eventually follow. Grim wasn't on the best of terms with the press lately, so I had at least a day or two before someone from the Afterlife Council leaked the news.

Then, Downy Dave from *Limbo Weekly* would start stalking me for the full story. I'd have to wait for Jenni's follow-up report to see just how much information I was allowed to share, but I didn't have a problem giving Dave an interview. Of all the press I'd received since rising up from the bottom of the barrel, Dave's articles were the only ones that painted me in a positive light. I needed contacts like him if I wanted my reputation to have a fighting chance among all the tabloid smut.

After my shower, I took a nap. It felt utterly selfish, even though I knew I'd earned it. The rest of my unit was out there, up to their eyeballs in souls, but I couldn't bring myself to leave the condo. My shoulders felt like they were dislocated from all the hellcat chopping, and the cuts on my ribcage itched something fierce. Besides, I had a date I needed to be well rested for.

I would wait for Jenni's report before talking to Downy Dave, but I was going to tell Bub tonight. Maybe it would cheer him up, and maybe it would keep Cindy Morningstar from stretching out the next Hell Committee meeting so long.

I woke around six, after five hours of fitful sleep. The condo was too quiet without the hounds' snores. Josie and Kevin weren't back yet, but with the lists I'd given them, it was no surprise. I would be off on my date with Bub before they finished delivering the day's catch, and it was just as well. If I were lucky, Jenni would fill them in before Josie had a chance to drill me for details.

I took another shower after I looked in the mirror and found that I'd missed some war paint. Then I slipped on a strapless, turquoise gown. It was a simple design, free of embellishments, with a full skirt that fell to my ankles. I chose a pair of silver flats to go with it since being comfortable was going to be challenging enough. My shoulders were burning in their sockets. I decided to schedule a morning appointment with the masseuse who worked at the Holly House gym.

Right as I finished my hair and makeup, Charlie called from the front desk to let me know that there was a limo waiting. Bub was ten minutes early, which was significantly better than being three hours late.

"Making up for lost time?" I greeted him with a kiss after we were tucked away behind the tinted windows.

"Something like that." Bub laughed and pulled me in tight against his chest. His attire was subtle tonight, a simple black tuxedo, but he still managed to look sinfully erotic.

"I was almost afraid Cindy would hijack my evening again, but fortunately, your boss called her away for an emergency council meeting."

"Well, he's not wasting any time."

Bub's eyes glowed in the dim light. "Do tell."

I turned into him, letting my breath linger on his neck as I lowered my voice to a whisper. "Caim is dead."

"What? How?" Bub's embrace went rigid. The carefree smile was gone, the laughter in his voice stifled.

The sudden shift gave me a chill, and I trembled in his arms. "I thought you'd be thrilled."

Bub blinked a few times and slowly loosened his hold on me. "I'm just surprised. When did this happen? *How* did it happen? He hasn't even been sighted since he fled the city."

I pulled away enough to make eye contact. "This morning. Jenni, Maalik, Gabriel, and I ambushed his ship out on the sea."

Bub's expression turned to stone. "Is there some reason why Maalik was included on this mission and I wasn't?"

I refrained from rolling my eyes. "Jenni organized everything. I didn't have any say in the details. You'd have to ask her."

He was silent for a painfully long moment. "Why didn't you tell me before you left? You could have died." The glow in his eyes softened to a dull smolder, keeping pace with his voice as it dissolved into nothing more than a quivering breath.

I put my hand over his and squeezed. "I didn't tell anyone. I couldn't. And I didn't die. I'm perfectly fine. Jenni was the one who took Caim out. I was nowhere near him."

Bub nodded, but I could tell he was far from appeased. He pulled me back in against his chest and rested his chin on top of my head. "I'm glad you're safe—" The ring of his cellphone blasted through the limo. He dug it out of his pocket and swore. "It's Cindy."

My heart deflated. "We're not going to dinner, are we?"

Bub pressed his lips together and answered on the second ring. "Yes?" he growled into the phone.

I couldn't hear Cindy's side of the conversation, but she clearly didn't have much to say. Bub ended the call without another word.

"I'm so sorry." He turned back to me with slumped shoulders and a defeated scowl.

I swallowed and tried to smile at him. "I know. It's okay. Maybe Monday after class?"

He nodded slowly. "Do you think you could sit in? Just for the first one. To let me know how I do."

"Sure."

Bub pressed an intercom button and told the driver to turn around. He apologized again before kissing me goodnight in front of Holly House. Then he sent the limo off and took the travel booth across the street to wherever Cindy had ordered him to go. I didn't bother asking. If I wanted him to respect my secrets, I had to start respecting his, too.

When I made it back upstairs to the condo, Jenni sat at the breakfast bar, stuffing her face with leftover Chinese takeout. She paused to give my dress a once-over and swallowed.

"Early dinner date?" she asked.

I plopped down next to her. "Canceled dinner date."

Jenni snorted and passed me a box of lo mein with a set of chopsticks. "And you all wonder why I'm single."

I poked at the noodles, but my appetite had fled with Bub's departure. "Enjoy the rest of your day?"

"Same as any other, I guess."

"You went back to work?" I gaped at her.

Jenni shrugged. "Why not?"

"Oh, I don't know. Maybe because you took out the second highest ranking general of the rebel forces this morning. Pretty sure that warrants an afternoon off, at the very least. A parade probably wouldn't be out of the question either."

Jenni shrugged again as if she hadn't just organized and executed the single most efficient and effective attack against the rebels so far.

"Your modesty is really fucking disturbing sometimes."

She grinned and raised an eyebrow at me. "I'm sure we've got some cookies around here if you need one."

"Screw the cookies. I've got a massage in the morning."

Keys jingled at the front door, and I stood with a gasp. Jenni frowned but quickly translated my anxiety.

"I'll have a follow-up report on your desk in the morning. In the meantime, let me take care of Josie's questions."

"No problem. I'm going to change." I waved a hand down at myself. "I'm not really interested in answering these questions either."

Jenni nodded, and I hurried off before the front door opened.

I didn't catch much of the conversation, but I did recognize the annoyed decibel of Josie's voice through my door. It eventually faded into subdued acceptance. I couldn't bring myself to face her yet, so I stayed shut up in my room for the rest of the evening, only opening my door long enough to let the hounds in.

I checked my email on the tablet. Jack had sent me a list of Bub's class roster. Kevin and Clair had both made the cut. A copy of the class syllabus and reading list were also attached. A quick read-through proved that Jack had been the one to write everything up. I couldn't help but feel annoyed on his behalf. All the things he did that Bub got credit for.

Before the evening grew too late, I did what I'd promised myself I would do if we survived the mission. I called the two remaining members of my generation and scheduled a meeting for Sunday night. Then I took a page from Jenni's book and pretended that it was an ordinary day. I brushed my teeth, tucked the hounds in, and went to bed early.

I didn't think about how the rebels were going to retaliate. I didn't think about the dinner I didn't get to have with Bub. And I most definitely didn't think about the questions I hadn't gotten the chance to ask Maalik about Winston. All of that could wait another day. Caim was dead. Jenni could be as modest as she wanted to be. I was going to celebrate, and I would start by getting a fantastic night's sleep, followed by a massage in the morning.

⚔

CHAPTER SEVEN

"Death will be a great relief.
No more interviews."
—Katharine Hepburn

Reapers Inc. was all abuzz on Saturday morning. Ellen stopped me before I made it to my desk and directed me immediately into Grim's office. It felt entirely too urgent to be anything as happy as a celebratory toast to a job well done.

"Close the door," Grim snapped as soon as I entered.

He sat behind his desk with mussed hair and minus his usual fancy suit jacket. The shades were drawn, and the room was thick with the musky smell of cigars. Jenni sat in one of the chairs before his desk, looking greener by the second.

"Take a seat, Harvey." Grim was nowhere near pleased.

Caim was dead, damn it. Was a little gratitude really too much for him to muster? I was suddenly furious.

"What's the problem? Did someone resurrect Caim?" I dropped into the chair next to Jenni with a scowl.

Grim huffed and pushed the sleeves of his dress shirt up to his elbows. "If someone had, at least we'd know who we're up against."

"It's been less than twenty-four hours." I glared at him. "You're seriously suggesting that the rebels already have a new general?"

Grim ground his teeth. "They only needed fifteen hours. Hypnos was abducted from Tartarus last night."

Jenni shook her head in disbelief. "They had to have this new general in place before our attack."

Grim slammed a fist on his desk. "It doesn't matter. We have to get Hypnos back. The water shipped in from his cave to the factory is no good if it's not infused by his presence."

I crossed my legs. "The Fates use a wide variety of purification methods as a precaution against threats like this. They should be fine."

Grim flushed a deep red. The muscles in his neck tensed as he loosened his tie with one hand. "I didn't call you in here for reassurance," he said through clenched teeth. "Your next assignment is to find and rescue Hypnos. Do you understand?"

Jenni stood. "Yes, sir. I'll start reaching out to contacts and gathering intel. You can expect a full report and mission draft by end of day."

"Dismissed. Both of you," he added, glancing my way.

I huffed and followed Jenni out. She grabbed my arm and pulled me down the hall, shutting us into my office.

"What's wrong with you?" she whispered with bulging eyes. "You can't talk to Grim that way. Are you *trying* to get terminated?"

I shrugged my arm out of her grasp. "He's not going to terminate me. Especially not with three reapers off the grid. You think he can afford to lose any more?"

Jenni shook her head. "I can't believe you've advanced this far with that attitude."

I raised an eyebrow and folded my arms. "Well, I guess there's just not enough room up Grim's ass for both of our heads, now is there?"

Jenni's gaze narrowed. "I'm going to pretend like you didn't say that." She stood taller, trying to reclaim some of the dignity I'd knocked out of her sails. "I'll have a new mission file for you tomorrow, after Grim's approval, of course."

"Of course," I echoed her.

Jenni gave up on our banter and stormed out of my office. We didn't butt heads often. It was an awkward encounter, and I hoped we didn't make a habit of it. I caught enough hell from Josie.

Thinking of Josie, I found the follow-up mission report on my desk. Grim's complete lack of enthusiasm made the whole thing seem pointless now. I decided to go ahead and take a look though, since Josie was bound to ask, and probably sooner rather than later. Plus, there was the Downy Dave interview I needed to be ready for.

I had twenty minutes before the morning meeting, so I skimmed the file. Then I filled out the soul dockets for the day, taking the less desirable harvests for myself. I felt sorry for the crappy lot I dealt out the day before, even more so, now that I'd been informed of how useless the mission had been.

I left the office to head for the harbor, but I barely made it to the sidewalk before the press swarmed me. They poured in from all sides, spilling out of cars and from behind bushes. The shock of it hit me like a grenade, and it was all I could do to pull my hand up over my face and clutch my duffle bag to my chest. Flashbulbs burned my eyes as a whole wave of questions poured out to me. They were too loud and jumbled to make sense of.

I considered retracing my steps back inside Reapers Inc., but then a green station wagon pulled up to the curb, breaking hard enough to squeal tires. Reporters knocked each other down to get out of the street in time.

"Get in!" Downy Dave was at the wheel. He pushed open the passenger door and waved me in.

I vaulted over a fallen photographer and threw myself into the front seat, slamming the door behind me. Dave swerved around the paparazzi. A female reporter from *Limbo's Laundry* flipped him the bird. He pushed his glasses up on his nose with his middle finger, returning the gesture with a grin.

The inside of Dave's car smelled like coffee and peppermint. The leather upholstery was scarred but otherwise clean. Dave was entirely too tidy and too nice to be a reporter.

"Thanks." I sighed and relaxed back in the seat.

"Don't thank me yet." He grinned sheepishly and pulled out a tape-recorder. "Do you mind?"

I had to laugh. "Not as long as you drop me off at the harbor."

"Deal." Dave clicked a button and set the recorder on the dash. His small wings fluttered, readjusting against the driver's seat. "Where to begin… let's see. Is it true that the rebel general Caim has been assassinated?"

"Yes." I nodded once.

Dave frowned at my curtness, but he continued. "And you were there to see this with your own eyes?"

"Yes." I nodded again.

"Can you give me a brief account of how it happened and what it felt like to be part of such a prominent turning point against the rebel forces?" Leave it to Dave to find a way around my simple approach.

"Jenni Fang organized an impeccable strategy. We found Caim at sea and ambushed his ship. I launched a distraction assault that Ms. Fang quickly followed with a swift execution. We were back in time for lunch."

"Wow." Dave gaped at me and bumped over a curb before pulling his eyes back to the road. "Wow," he repeated. "You make it sound like it was any other day. I would have been terrified. I've read the reports of Caim's ship. It's nothing to sneeze at."

I nodded. "I *was* terrified, but nothing is ever accomplished by ignoring things that frighten you."

Dave smiled encouragingly. "Good. That's good. The public needs to know you're human—well, as human as a reaper can get anyway. The success of the mission already proves you're brave. Now we need to give them something relatable, something they can use to feel good about themselves."

I sniffed. "I could be wrong here, though I'm definitely not complaining, but I thought reporters were supposed to seek out dark, exploitive bits that made readers gasp."

Dave's nose crinkled. "Sure. I guess if your writing sucks, that's always something to fall back on. Fortunately, I have a bit more confidence than that. Also, it's hard to get more interviews out of people once you've thrown them to the wolves."

"I like you, Dave. You're pretty all right."

"I am, aren't I? You're not too bad yourself." His wings fluttered as he puffed his chest out with a dopey, proud smile. "Okay, where were we?"

"Making me sound human so readers can feel good about themselves."

"Right. So, did you suffer any wounds in this battle?"

"Nothing fatal."

Dave groaned. "Give me something people can offer you sympathy over."

"Well." I tilted my head to one side. "A hellcat did take a swipe at my ribcage. Left a few scratches behind, but I didn't need stitches or anything."

"Good. Now we're getting somewhere."

By the time we made it to the harbor, Dave had asked me enough of the right questions to write a feature article. I wasn't keen on seeing my face on the cover of *Limbo Weekly*, especially since the story felt like it should have been built around Jenni. I asked him to hold off until I could beg her to give him an interview, which he happily agreed to. Like I said, way too nice for a reporter.

I thanked him again and asked a question of my own as I hopped out of his car. "How did everyone find out about Caim's death so quickly?"

Dave blinked at me. "Grim sent out a press release last night."

"Grim? You're sure?"

"First one in months. Guess he was waiting for some good news to share." He waved as he pulled away.

I hadn't expected Grim to leak the news so soon, but with Hypnos missing, it made sense. It was a perfect distraction. He was probably hoping we would find Hypnos and return him to Tartarus before anyone even realized he was gone.

Something felt different about this new mission. I couldn't understand why Grim was so torn up over a lesser god's disappearance. I'd been right about the Fates and their fail-safe purification system. This was just a hiccup. It hardly seemed to warrant cigars and a bad hair day.

Thanks to the paparazzi and Downy Dave taking the long way to the harbor, I was running late for the morning meeting. I found the rest of the Posy Unit waiting for me on the main deck of the ship, all sporting tired eyes full of dread. Their moods were only mildly improved after they reviewed the soul dockets I passed out.

Josie lingered around until everyone else had coined off, including Kevin, who I'd sent ahead on a cakewalk harvest. A dozen senior citizens who had perished due to a nursing home gas leak seemed manageable enough. I had him take the hounds, just in case.

"Was that Downy Dave who dropped you off this morning?" Josie asked, following me to the captain's cabin.

"Yeah." I laughed. "He saved me from being eaten alive by the press outside the office."

Josie sneered and leaned against the doorframe while I changed into my work robe. "And he did this out of the kindness of his little ol' heart, did he?"

"Nope." I sighed, already boring of her sour mood. "I gave up my pound of flesh in the form of an interview on the way here."

"I'll just bet you did." Josie folded her arms.

I dropped my duffle bag in the corner and sat on the edge of the bed to tighten my boot laces. "Okay. How 'bout we skip ahead to the part where you let me have it. I've got a docket full of shit harvests, so I'm a little pressed for time."

Josie's mouth puckered into an angry bow, but the effect was lost when her chin began to tremble. "All the secrets you've trusted me with, and you really thought you couldn't share the fact that you were taking off to ambush Caim's ship yesterday?"

I tilted my head back and zeroed in on the cabin ceiling with a groan. "Why is no one getting the *top-secret* bit about this mission?"

"That didn't stop you from telling me that you killed a deity last year or that your mere existence is a breach of the peace treaty."

"Keep it down," I hissed at her.

Josie threw her hands up. "You know what? Forget it. My harvest list actually looks decent for a change, and I'm not going to waste the day trying to figure out why my two best friends have suddenly decided I'm not good enough to tag along on their secret missions."

"Josie—"

She stormed out of the cabin and down the ship ramp, coining off as soon as she stepped onto the pier. Guilt slithered through me uninvited. I found myself resenting not only the rules I used to ignore, but also Josie, who had spent a good deal of our friendship quoting the rules every time I stumbled over one.

I sleepwalked through the rest of the day, collecting souls with the detached and foreboding demeanor commonly accepted as Death's proper aura. Even Kevin stayed out of my way, casting sideways glances and making short, safe statements only when necessary. He didn't question my secretiveness or pout about not being included on the mission. A year into his apprenticeship, and he had seen more atypical action than most reapers would expect in a century. He was also seeing more coin than the average reaper—apprentice or otherwise—thanks to his proxy placement on the Posy Unit. I wasn't sure whether to be concerned or proud of the fact that his ambition hadn't staled and he was eager to pad his resume with more classes at the academy.

I had other reasons for being glad Kevin had been left behind on Jenni's mission. The siren I'd encountered while fending off a hellcat had recognized me and remembered Kevin. It took me a while, but I remembered her now too, though in a more fishy form. She had been one of Eurynome's mermaids who had attacked us in the Pacific Ocean while we were on a harvest over the summer. This particular fiend had rendered Kevin deaf with her song, and I had to take him to Meng Po for one of her special healing teas.

I shouldn't have been surprised to find the sea sirens among Caim's shipmates. Eurynome had tried to kill me, for nothing more than feeling slighted by Beelzebub's accusation that she'd stolen the Helm of Hades. Still, Eurynome would make a poor general for the rebels. While her sirens could trade their fins for legs, she was bound to the sea. She also seemed more interested in playing in the mortal waters, rather than taking over any bodies of water in Eternity.

Kevin and I made it back to the ship with the hounds by late afternoon. At least my brooding had paid off in the form of efficiency. After sending a few dozen souls into the sea, we secured the rest of our catch in the hold. Kevin took a chance and stopped me outside the captain's cabin after I'd changed out of my work robe.

"Got a minute, boss?" he asked meekly.

"For what?"

Kevin tucked his hands inside the pockets of his robe. "Just thought you might like to see your new cabin."

"It's finished? Wait, I thought the new cabin was for you and Josie."

"Well, we're on the ship more often than you these days, so it made more sense for our cabin to be near center deck."

"Okay." I followed him out of the captain's cabin and down the side hall to the cabin set deeper into the ship's stern.

It had been some time since I'd last wandered this far from the familiar parts of the boat. It reminded me of how most humans avoided their attics and crawlspaces, though the disagreeable parts of my ship claimed the heftier side of the square footage ratio.

The passage we took was strewn with sheetrock-dusted cobwebs. They clung to the oval windows set into the ship's outer wall, dampening our only source of light. I hoped my new cabin was tidier, and brighter. I could take a mop to the hall later.

Kevin stopped at a shiny new door with an engraved nameplate.

Captain Lana Harvey
of the O'Malley Ghost Ship
Esteemed leader of the Posies
Slayer of Rebel Scum

If Kevin was shooting for brownie points, he could have them all. I squeezed his shoulder. "The force is strong with you, Padawan."

"Wait until you see the inside." His eyes sparkled as he pushed the door open.

The back cabin, which I had to call by its appropriate name now, the *great* cabin, was majestic. Crown molding framed the ceiling. The floor had been repaired with new boards and polished with a fresh coat of lacquer. White curtains spilled down from each corner and on either side of the French doors that led out to a narrow balcony facing the sea. A full-sized bed rested against the back wall that separated the room from the old cabin. It was made up with a matching white comforter and pillows. The far starboard wall featured a small desk, lit by more oval windows like the ones in the hallway.

Kevin picked at the hem of his sleeve and chewed his bottom lip. "Do you like it?"

I hardly knew what to say. "Are you sure that you and Josie shouldn't have this cabin? It's really wonderful, but you said it yourself, you two spend far more time on board than I do."

"No, really, it's fine." He waved off my concerns. "This was a test run. I'm redoing the forecastle cabin for me and Josie. It should be done some time next week."

"Oh. Good." At least that would save me from another one of Josie's guilt trips.

"So…" Kevin's brows lifted, waiting for my final assessment.

"It's amazing. You did a fantastic job. In fact, I'm going to start spending more time on the ship now, just because of this room. Thank you. Seriously."

Kevin laughed. "I'm glad you like it. I finished it early, because I wanted to thank you for getting me into Bub's class. And don't worry. I'll tell anyone who asks—and plenty of people who don't ask—that you insisted I take the course."

The mention of Bub soured my mood, but that wasn't Kevin's fault. I gave him a strained smile. "Thanks. I better head back to the office and get this paperwork filed."

"Hey." Kevin stopped me as I turned around. "Don't tell Josie, but I'm really glad she didn't go on that mission with you. I know she's angry and feeling left out right now, but I'm sure some part of her is relieved too."

"Yeah, a very tiny part of her that she's not likely to claim any time soon."

"Even so." He frowned softly. "We weren't made to be foot soldiers. Our creed and entire existence centers on us being psychopomps, guiding souls over from the mortal realm."

"You don't need to quote Reaping 101 to me, pilgrim. Jenni, maybe. Trust me. I'm perfectly content harvesting souls."

I was pretty sure I'd never uttered those words out loud before. But, given the option between my typical job and slaying demons, I was rather fond of the life expectancy the former offered.

As lovely as Kevin's surprise had been, I was ready to get off the ship before Josie returned. I considered it lucky that we hadn't run into each other in between harvests while dropping souls off in the hold. I wasn't ready to see her again so soon, and I really wanted to talk to Jenni first to see how she was handling Josie's resentment. Or maybe her grudge was for me alone.

In my haste, I ran into Asmodeus as he stepped on board the ship. We collided so hard that his blue fedora was knocked right off his head, and I would have been knocked right on my ass, if he hadn't caught my arm.

"I realize I'm known for sweeping ladies off their feet, but I assure you, I have better methods." He laughed nervously and released my arm.

"It was my fault. I wasn't watching." I snatched up his hat and dusted it off before handing it back to him.

Asmodeus was Bub's best friend, but I didn't see him often. He didn't care for politics or Bub's elaborate parties. Being a lust demon had lost its magic for him, and he was taking a sabbatical, so to speak. He had still come to Bub's aid when Caim and Loki held me hostage at the Fates' factory over the summer, and all he had to show for it was a nasty scar under his left shoulder blade, where Caim had stabbed him with Atropos' shears.

"What brings you to the harbor today?"

"I wanted to check in on your lover boy." He gave me a silly grin and glanced around the ship. "Isn't he here with you?"

"Uh, no," I answered slowly.

"He was supposed to meet me for lunch. I ran into Amy, and she said he missed the Hell Committee meeting this morning too—" he stopped short, noticing my worry.

"That can't be good."

"I'm sure it's nothing," he added quickly, running a hand through his hair before putting his hat on. "I can't think of many reasons he'd go off the grid, but I was sure you were at the top of the list."

"I thought I was too." This was getting uncomfortable. "I'm supposed to meet him at the academy Monday night to sit in on his first class."

Asmodeus nodded. "Right. The demon defense course." He clapped his hands together. "Bub's probably busy preparing lesson plans." He sounded about as convinced as I felt.

"Sure. I bet that's it."

"If you see him before I do, tell the prick to call, yeah?"

I nodded.

Asmodeus walked down the ship ramp with me. Then he stopped before we parted ways. "Maybe you could tell that roommate of yours to call too." He grinned and handed me one of his cards.

"Still pining over Jenni, are we?" I smiled and tucked his card in my duffle bag.

He winked. "A guy can dream."

CHAPTER EIGHT

I didn't try to call Bub Saturday night. I would not be that nagging girlfriend who demanded to know his location at all times. Besides, I couldn't offer him the same in return, and my perception of fairness already felt skewed thanks to Josie's blowup. I spent another night confined to my room with only the hounds for company.

Sunday morning, I found a new mission file on my desk. I glanced over it before the morning meeting and decided that Jenni had forgiven me. We would be doing recon work on Monday, with minimal chance of encountering demons. I could live with that. Kevin's statement about our psychopomp purpose was still weighing on my mind, and I wanted to hear what Jenni thought of it. I also needed to ask her about Josie, who had decided to shift gears and give me the silent treatment. I made this new discovery at the morning meeting.

As much as I wanted to take Kevin with me to harvest again, I sent him with Josie, hoping he would put in a good word for me, or at least improve her mood. I had a lot on my mind anyway, and harvesting with the hounds gave me the needed silence to sort through my thoughts.

I finished up the workday late and had to skip changing out of my robe in order to make it across town in time for my meeting with Mira and Ben, the two other remaining reapers of my generation.

Mira Hart was what I liked to call a cookie-cutter reaper. She was medium height, medium build, with medium length, wavy, black hair. She harvested medium-risk souls, collected medium-grade pay, and lived in Reapers Tower, a medium-range apartment complex in Limbo City. Nothing about Mira was under or overstated. She didn't cause trouble, and she didn't draw attention. She was the predictable kind of reaper that Grim probably preferred.

Mira had agreed to meet with me in the lobby café of Reapers Tower. I would have invited her to Holly House, but there were fewer prying eyes and ears on her side of the city. Ben Holt would be joining us too, though I had a feeling he would be running late.

Calling Ben the opposite of Mira was too harsh. He really did try. A lot harder than I used to anyway. He was still collecting low-risk souls, despite his efforts to nab a promotion. He'd even taken some extra courses at the academy, not that he'd scored overly well. Ben had been the lowest-ranking graduate of our generation. That wasn't saying much, though, seeing as how there had only been six of us. Five, if I didn't count the *unexisted* Craig Hogan.

Still, Ben had plenty of admirable characteristics. For starters, he lacked Craig Hogan's malicious ambition and

Vince Hare's mindless greed. Which probably meant that he was in no real danger of being recruited by the rebels. Today's meeting was mostly so I could dig for information on Tasha Henry.

Mira and I went ahead and ordered coffee while we waited for Ben. Then we found a corner table near a window that overlooked a small wooded area on the northern edge of Limbo City. Before we sat down, Mira surprised me with a hug.

"It's so good to see you," she said, climbing onto one of the tall barstools.

"Yeah. You, too." I gave her an awkward smile.

Mira and I hadn't talked much since our apprenticeships ended, but her friendliness was genuine. It didn't stink of ambition and pursuit like Craig's had.

Mira folded her hands over the table. "So, I'm taking a stab in the dark here and guessing this meeting has something to do with Tasha Henry's disappearance?"

My smile tightened. "I wish it were under better circumstances." I cupped my hands around my coffee and sighed.

Mira nodded. "Yeah. Me, too." She tucked a lock of hair behind her ear and looked out the window. "I don't know how much help I'll be. I went running with Tasha twice a week, up until three months ago."

"What happened three months ago?"

"She started dating a demon." Mira bit her lip and shot me an apologetic glance. "I'm not prejudiced. I didn't stop running with her. She stopped running with me."

"Did she say why?"

Mira shook her head. "I guess she was too busy being wooed. She spent every free minute at his place."

"Did he live in the city?" I asked.

"In one of the apartments over on the west side. She invited me to a party there a few weeks ago, but I didn't stay long. The neighborhood's unsavory enough, and I tried to be open-minded, but the company wasn't too hot either—well, you know what I mean."

"What was this demon's name?"

"Tasha called him Tack. I think she said he had a business visa. Something to do with delivering building supplies for the new travel booths. Does that help?"

Her question threw me. I sat back in my chair. "I don't know, but I'll pass it along to Jenni Fang."

Mira grinned. "I read the *Reaper Report,* you know."

I had forgotten about the press release. Shit. I'd need to stop by a newsstand on the way home. I gave Mira a blank look. "I haven't seen the *Reaper Report* yet today."

Her eyes widened. "You and Jenni Fang are on the cover."

Well, that helped explain Josie's extra frosty attitude this morning.

Mira shivered and hugged herself. "I used to think I wanted to advance beyond medium-risk harvests. I'm not so sure anymore."

I grimaced. "Yeah, I don't know that the notoriety is worth the shortened life expectancy. It's a little late for me to toss in the towel now, though."

Mira nodded sympathetically.

"Heya, ladies." Ben plopped down on the stool between us with a giant mug of hot chocolate. A tuft of black hair stuck out from under the clasp of his backward ball cap. He was ten minutes late, but he'd found time to change out of his work robe, unlike Mira and me.

"What'd I miss?" he asked, dripping hot chocolate onto his polo shirt and the table.

Mira's nose crinkled as she edged away from him. "We were just talking about Tasha Henry's disappearing act. Know anything about it?"

Ben slurped at his drink. "I used to see her at the dock all the time. She shared a yacht with Karen Durst."

"That's right." Mira nodded. "Though hardly surprising."

A light bulb flickered in the back of my mind. Josie would have to hate me a little longer. I had a lot to talk to Jenni about tonight. Maybe we could schedule a secret meeting in the gym sauna so we wouldn't have to worry about Josie brooding in the next room.

I took my time finishing my coffee, letting Mira and Ben amble through the small talk and catching up that was long overdue. We reminisced over our first days at the academy and shared stories about our apprenticeships and subsequent harvesting placements. I glazed over my timeline, not wanting to toot my own horn since all the rags in town seemed to be tooting it for me.

I excused myself around eight, much later than I had planned to stay. Mira jumped up to offer me another hug that I accepted more gracefully this time.

Ben shook my hand with a playfully staunch face. "Safe travels, Captain Harvey."

"Aye, Mr. Holt. And safe travels to you, too," I replied.

We parted with grins and promises to meet again soon.

I took the travel booth down the street from Reapers Tower to the one near Holly House. The sky had grown dark, but the air was alive along Divine Boulevard. Lazy tendrils of smoke glowed in the streetlights. An exiled faerie had recently set up shop across the intersection from Holly House. The sign simply said *Little Folk Shoppe*, and a placard below advertised that they sold oils, incense, and magical trinkets.

The smell was intoxicating. It even rivaled the buttery garlic aroma of the pizza joint situated on the other side of Memorial Drive. I paused to enjoy the contrast and noticed a hooded figure stepping out of the store, carrying a small gift-wrapped box.

"Winston?" My mouth went dry.

I glanced behind me to the travel booth where a lone nephilim guard stood watch. If Grim got reports from the booth guards, he was not going to like this one. I took my chances and sprinted across the street, snagging Winston's arm and pulling him around the backside of the Little Folk Shoppe before he could say a word.

"Nice to see you, too," he grumbled.

"What the hell are doing out here?" I scanned the alley to make sure we were alone.

The dumpsters were hidden by a stone wall that bordered a patio behind the store, and a tiny garden filled the space. A rainbow of daisies and lilies spilled from hanging pots and giant planters, and vines and ornamental grass had been braided together to form a canopy over an old bench.

Winston yanked his arm free with a huff. "Relax. I look like an ordinary soul to everyone else. In fact, I *am* an ordinary soul. Remember?"

"Does Grim know that?" I snapped.

"Of course not. You're alive, aren't you?"

"Not for much longer if he spots you strolling around the city," I all but shouted at him.

"Take a deep breath. Grim has already checked in with me for the evening." He paused. "I take that back. He checked in with Naledi."

I gasped. "I thought you said—"

Winston held a hand up. "Naledi is a true original believer. She can do more than I ever dreamed of doing on the throne. Khadija probably could have too, and I imagine her modesty—more than anything—is what allowed her influence over Eternity to last as long as it did. Naledi can manipulate her own essence and take my form. Grim is none the wiser."

My blood pressure dropped back into a safe range. I leaned against the building and blew out a tense breath. "What about Maalik? Does he know about this?"

Winston turned away from me. He seemed irritated any time I pried for a full report, but he had to understand my concern when my life hung in the balance. If Grim found out that Winston had stepped down from the throne and installed a new soul, he would lose it. If he found out that I had anything to do with finding that new soul... The secret torture chamber on the thirty-seventh floor of Reapers Inc. came to mind, and I shivered.

"Maalik doesn't know either," Winston finally confessed. "He doesn't know about Naledi, period. I'd like to keep it that way." He gave me a hard look.

"You seem pretty taken by this girl, trying to keep her all to yourself. Is that why you haven't replaced my coin to the throne realm?"

"I'd take away Maalik's coin too if I wasn't so worried that he'd find it suspicious. I make Grim go through Coreen's memorial statue still, but he doesn't care to be out in public that often. He only visits about once or twice a week, and usually just to make sure I haven't been abducted by rebels."

"The memorial statue still works?"

"Only for Grim."

"I know about Naledi, and you know I don't have it in my schedule to bother you often. Why wouldn't you want me having access to the throne realm?"

Winston pressed his lips together like he was sure he had already said more than he should have. I could see his thoughts shifting around carefully before he spoke again. "Naledi is…different. She's special, and I don't mean just to me. She should be handled carefully."

"I don't understand. You think I would upset her or something?" My brow furrowed, and I took a step back.

"Maybe not intentionally," Winston said. "But it's best not to risk it yet. She's still adapting to the throne, and I'm trying to help her as best I can."

I eyeballed the package in his hands. "By buying her trinkets?"

He blushed. "It's incense. She finds it soothing."

"So…what? You're her errand boy?"

"And what if I am?" He was angry now.

"I'm sorry. It's been a rough few days. I imagine you heard about Caim?"

"I did. Congratulations," he said somberly. "But I'm afraid your victory will be short-lived."

"I guess you've heard about Hypnos too, then."

He nodded. "Among other things. There's a disturbance in the sea. Not a rogue island like Khadija's decline produced, but something else."

"That's nice and vague." I folded my arms.

Winston lowered his eyes and cradled the gift for Naledi close to his stomach. "The rebels are aligning themselves quickly and quietly now. It is not in the throne's power to thwart their efforts, nor can the throne shine light on *every* element at play." His eyes flicked up to mine.

"But?" I offered. I could feel something dark and awful lingering in his unspoken words.

"The things Naledi has seen are not for me to share. I don't think I could make you believe them anyway. Please, be careful. War is filled with slights of hand, and no matter the victor, everyone loses something."

"War? A few terrorist attempts hardly count as war."

Winston wet his lips. "I've said too much, and I've stayed too long."

He glanced down the alley and fetched a coin from his pocket. It was one of the rare ones he had made before giving up the throne. It bypassed the wards Grim had enforced on the city after the travel booths were installed.

"How am I supposed to get in touch with you?" I asked.

"You're not." His hard features softened. "But we'll meet again soon." He flipped the coin and was gone.

CHAPTER NINE

"We dance round in a ring and suppose,
while the secret sits in the middle and knows."
—Robert Frost

Everyone was in bed by the time I made it home. Even the hounds. I couldn't sleep, though I gave it my best. My mind was full of questions. I tossed and turned until I heard Josie and Kevin leave for the gym. Then I fired up the coffee pot and fed the hounds.

Josie had left the recruits file on the kitchen counter with two resumes paper-clipped to the front of it. I could tell she was still pulling the silent treatment since there wasn't a note accompanying her selection.

Molly Driver, Josie's first pick, was a fourth-generation, high-risk harvester. Her resume showed that she had been passed over for the Mother Goose Unit because she hadn't scored high enough on her sensitivity test. She'd aced it, but the reaper who was chosen over her had scored two points higher. That sucked. If she had opted for an open placement instead of exclusively applying for the Mother Goose Unit, she would have fared better at the placement ceremony.

Molly was older and more experienced than anyone else on the Posy Unit. It made me wonder if Josie had chosen her to spite me. I abandoned the thought after I saw her second choice. Tyler Ives was a ninth-generation, medium-risk harvester. He not only fit the young and eager-to-please profile Josie had suggested, but his academy transcript was very impressive. Also, his apprenticeship had been under Coreen Bendura, one of the highest honors among reapers.

I was on my third cup of coffee when Jenni finally shuffled into the kitchen. She had bags under her eyes, and her cheeks were flushed with the unmistakable puffiness only brought on by a good cry.

"I thought you'd be sleeping better—all things considered." I hopped up to fix her a cup of coffee.

"That was the plan. Someone forgot to tell my psyche that Caim's dead." Jenni slumped down on a barstool and rubbed her temples with a groan.

I didn't want to be insensitive, but I had too much I needed to talk to her about. I figured I had already compromised by not waking her up in the middle of the night to unload, so I gave her an apologetic smile and jumped right in.

"I talked to Mira and Ben last night. Tasha shared a yacht with Karen Durst, and she was dating a demon named Tack, who lived over on the west side."

Jenni took a long drink of her coffee, glaring at me over the rim of her cup. When she set it down, she cleared her throat. "I know. Where do you think we're going today?"

"Sorry." I cringed but didn't let her morning gruff discourage me. "Just a couple more things I need to run by you."

"Use as few words as possible," she grumbled, standing to top off her mug.

"Downy Dave would like an interview. You really should talk to him, because he's probably the only reporter who will say anything nice about us. Kevin suggested that we're not cut out for special ops. That it's not in our psychopomp nature. I'd like to hear your thoughts on that. Josie is off-the-charts pissed at me. I'm curious if you're getting the cold shoulder too, and how you suggest I—or we—deal with it. Oh! And Asmodeus asked me to give you his card. He first laid eyes on you while you were unconscious and covered in blood. Make of that what you will. My personal assessment is that nice guys have the weirdest fetishes."

The last bit of my spiel caught Jenni off guard, and she overfilled her mug. "Well, I'm awake now." She wiped the counter down and then turned to place both hands on the breakfast bar between us. "I don't care how nice you think Dave is. He's a reporter, and therefore, cannot be trusted. If he wants to ask questions, he can email them. I like my answers to be calculated, and I'd like Grim's publicist to go over them first."

"Fair enough."

"If you're worried about the missions I'm taking you on, I suggest you train harder. If you're up for it, you're welcome to spar with me at the dojo Tuesday and Thursday evenings. And, yes, Josie is snubbing me, too. It's not that I don't find her competent, but Grim wouldn't allow me to leave the Posy Unit so handicapped. I chose you over her for obvious reasons, and I'm not sorry. In other words, I have absolutely no idea how to smooth things over."

"Me either. Great." I yawned and ran a hand over my face.

Jenni shrugged and finished off her second cup of coffee. She went to fill a third, speaking with her back to me. "And you can keep the demon's calling card. I have four of them. Persistent bastard."

"What do you have against Asmodeus?"

Jenni paused. "It's not that he isn't charming enough, but I'm really not up for the media shitstorm. Grim would have a fit too, and I have to work too closely with him to worry about that kind of backlash."

I nodded, wishing I had her level-headedness when it came to matters of the heart. I wouldn't have traded Bub to appease Grim, but Jenni was right. The media shitstorm was no picnic.

Jenni reclaimed her seat and gave me a bored frown. "I'd like to get caffeinated in peace now, if you don't mind."

I left her alone in the kitchen and took an early shower. Since I was taking half the day off, the soul dockets would need to be sorted out more strategically. Plus, I hadn't stopped by a newsstand yet, but Ellen was sure to have a copy of the *Reaper Report* Mira had mentioned.

Saul and Coreen whimpered at me as I dressed. I relied on Josie and Kevin to take care of them a lot lately, and while the hounds seemed to like my roommates well enough, I couldn't blame them for feeling neglected. Since I'd made captain, I'd been spending more time at Reapers Inc., where Grim had made it perfectly clear that the hounds were not welcome.

It had only been a few days since the news of Caim's death and my involvement had hit the streets, but it was stale enough for the likes of Limbo City. I wore my robe to work with the hood up, just in case. After Jenni returned Dave's email and he published the full story, I would be in the clear again.

Ellen met me as I stepped off the elevator. "Thank the gods you're here. Please, help me."

Something slammed against the inside of Grim's office door. Muffled swearing followed. Then something else shattered. It sounded as if he were interviewing a wrecking ball with Tourette's.

I raised an eyebrow at Ellen. "What do you suggest?"

"I don't know. Something. Anything. I've been his secretary for a thousand years, and I've never seen him like this." Her eyes watered as she pleaded with me.

"Look, I've never been very good at improving Grim's mood. Jenni should be here soon." I glanced up at the clock on the wall and tried to guesstimate how much damage Grim could do in the next ten minutes. "Maybe we should hide out in my office until she gets here."

Ellen glanced back at her desk and then jumped as something else broke in the next room. "Okay."

"Do you have yesterday's *Reaper Report?*"

Ellen grabbed a stack of magazines off her desk, along with a box of chocolates she had stashed under her keyboard, and we hurried down the hall to my office.

Once we were safely inside, she tossed the magazines on my desk and collapsed in one of the guest chairs. "What's wrong with him?"

"Beats the hell outta me." I clicked on my desk lamp and shuffled through the magazines until I found the *Reaper Report*.

The cover was a spliced image. One side was a picture of Jenni, taken the day of the placement ceremony when she was announced as Grim's new second-in-command. The other side was a shot of me from Saturday morning's media assault outside Reapers Inc. My mouth was hanging open, and one eye squinted in the harsh camera light. The photographers never failed to capture my most unflattering moments. Their professionalism was seriously lacking…which is probably how they'd landed their jobs in the first place.

Ellen stuffed a chocolate into her mouth and tried to talk around it. "The article's not so bad in that one. They pretty much stuck to the press release."

I grunted and flipped through the stack until I found a copy of *Limbo's Laundry*. Jenni and I were on the cover again, but Jenni took up more space this time. A photoshopped collage of her at the placement ceremony, the harbor, and the dojo stretched across most of the page, with only a small image of me in the bottom right corner. It was an old picture taken at the Hearth from one of my dinner dates with Bub. He had been left out of the photo, leaving me looking very secret-agentish in a slinky black dress and high heels, stepping out of a limo.

The headlines were cheesy, as always. The larger one over Jenni's spread read *From Victim to Victor: Grim's New Second is*

Back in the Saddle. My caption read *Does Grim's Second Have a Second of her Own?*

It seemed a little odd that Caim's death hadn't been mentioned more directly. That should have been the bigger news of the week. Or year. Leave it to the tabloids to skip right over that and focus on gossipy speculation and personal details that were none of their business.

Ellen mumbled something and waved her hand at me. She swallowed her chocolate and tried again. "The pictures are nice, but the article in that one is a bunch of crap. Three sentences from the press release, used out of context, and a heap of nonsense."

"Typical."

She shrugged and held the box of chocolates out to me. I took one and popped it into my mouth with a huff. I'd saved *Limbo Weekly* for last. Downy Dave had promised to hold off on publishing the feature article until he heard from Jenni, and their magazine came out on Wednesdays anyway. The press release had been sent out Friday night after Grim had been informed about Hypnos. Just in time for *Limbo's Laundry* to slap together a new cover story for the newsstands on Saturday morning.

Ellen finished off the last of her chocolates and gave the box a wounded pout. "I don't think I have enough treats to get me through the day. Do you really think Jenni can help with Grim?"

"More than I can. I'm pretty sure just looking at me gives Grim ulcers." I grinned and rummaged around in my desk until I found a few candy bars and handed them over. They had been Ellen's to begin with, gifted to me on a bad day.

Ellen's answer to all of life's pains—and joys for that matter—was chocolate. She pretended to loathe the extra curves she'd acquired from this habit, but that didn't stop her from indulging. It didn't stop her from wearing snug pencil skirts either. Though her fuller figure did seem to enhance the fifties and sixties fashions she was drawn to. The style looked especially appropriate on her today, paired with my outdated office furniture.

The two guest chairs looked like Ikea rejects, with crooked legs and peeling vinyl cushions. One was dark green, and the other looked like it might have been at one time. It sat closer to the window and had seen too many sunny days. Grim's jab at my décor crept back to me, and I frowned.

"You know any good decorators?"

Ellen grinned. "I'm sure I can make a few phone calls."

"Oh," I added, digging the recruits file out of my duffle bag. "Grim wanted some names from me today."

Ellen took the file and glanced over the reapers Josie had picked out. "I'll get the paperwork ready, but no promises for when Grim will get around to signing off on them."

As if on cue, more smashing and crashing filtered through the thin walls.

"I might not be the only one you have to call a decorator for this week."

Jenni burst into my office. "Time to go," she said, shooting Ellen a scowl. "Before Grim takes down the entire building."

"You can't leave me here alone with him like that. You were supposed to make it better," Ellen whined.

"The only thing that's going to make it better is some good news, and I'm hoping to have some for him by lunch." Jenni turned her nose up and hurried off.

I grabbed my duffle bag and slipped past Ellen, patting her arm on my way out the door. "I'll bring back some more sweets," I whispered before sprinting down the hall to catch up with Jenni.

Once we were safely shut in the elevator and on our way down, Jenni turned to me. "Why do you associate so heavily with Grim's secretary? You are aware she holds no influence over him, right?" Her harshness startled me.

"Not all of my associations are for personal gain. Ellen's nice, and she helps me out a lot."

Jenni raised an eyebrow. "Yeah, a lot more than she helps any of the other captains out. Don't think they haven't noticed."

"Maybe if they were nicer to her, she'd help them more, too. I don't see why I should be rude just to fit in. I'm the odd duck out anyway, so what's it matter?"

Jenni harrumphed as the elevator opened on the first floor. We walked out of the building together, and only then did I realize what a stupid move that had been. A camera flashed from the window of a car pulling away from the curb.

Jenni shook her head. "Great. Looks like we'll be making headlines for another week."

"Email Dave those interview answers, and they'll back off." I slung my bag over my shoulder. "Where should I find you after my unit meeting?"

"We'll start at the harbor. Tasha and Karen's yacht."

"It's still there?"

Jenni nodded. "Guess the rebels were afraid it could be tracked. Some of the newer transports have GPS systems registered with Reapers Inc. in case they go missing at sea. It's a lot more common lately, considering all the rebel attacks."

We parted ways before reaching my ship. We hadn't planned it, but it was clearly a mutual move to steady the waters with Josie. She didn't look quite as angry this morning, but she was still in silent mode.

Kate and Alex played fetch with the hounds, while Kevin attempted to hold a conversation with Arden. Even the daunting African Posy was more talkative than Josie today.

Between Ellen's crisis with Grim, and Jenni's eagerness to get the hell out of dodge, I hadn't found time to sort out the soul dockets. Making everyone sing for their harvests would be one way to get Josie to crack. The unit circled round as I came on board.

I pulled out the harvest list and cleared my throat. "I've got a war zone, a prison riot, and an apartment fire, and then we'll all meet up for a bombing this afternoon."

Kate was quick to nab the easiest job for her and Alex. "Prison riot."

"War zone," Kevin jumped in, trading a look with Josie before turning to Arden. "If that's okay with you."

Arden nodded, silently claiming the apartment fire. I had a feeling he would have chosen it anyway if given first pick. That harvest was most likely to have a few child souls. Arden had worked on the Mother Goose Unit before joining the Posies, and though he had willingly switched teams, he seemed to miss working with children. I think he preferred their awe and eagerness to believe.

Adult souls were definitely harder to convince of their demise. In the modern world, skepticism grew on souls like mildew. It started to drop off some after a mortal reached their seventies. I'd once harvested a man on his ninety-fourth birthday, who'd lectured me for taking so long, blaming me for everything from his cataracts to his leaky bladder.

Josie and Kevin waited for the others to coin off. The hounds were wagging around, waiting for a command from one of us. They could travel by coin, but they had to be standing up against someone's leg to do so. Kevin cleared his throat and flicked an uneasy gaze between Josie and me. He was not enjoying being the middleman.

"Are we taking the hounds today?" he asked.

Josie didn't move, but I could tell she was paying attention now. I hadn't claimed a harvest from the morning docket. If I sent the hounds with them, it would be a big flashing sign that I had other plans, and it wouldn't take a tabloid minion to speculate that those plans probably involved some secret mission with Jenni Fang.

"No," I answered quickly. "I'll take them with me."

Kevin nodded. I whistled to the hounds, beckoning them to follow me back to my new cabin, where I hoped Josie would assume I was dropping off my bag—not waiting for them to leave. I gave it five minutes and then left with the hounds to find Jenni.

Tasha and Karen's yacht was docked on the outer pier. A yellow notice tacked to their dock post advertised to the world that they were late on their boat slip rent. It was dated a week before Tasha had disappeared. It was probably difficult for her to keep up with the payments after Karen had split.

I made my way up to the yacht's stern deck and found Jenni inspecting the lock on the first-tier entrance. The door looked solid. I spent half a second wondering if she had some secret agent lock-picking skills when she suddenly stood and kicked the door in, splintering it in half. The hounds both yipped in surprise.

"Well. That's one way to do it."

Jenni ignored me and stepped around her carnage to get inside.

Tasha and Karen's boat was modest by luxury yacht standards. The lower level, which had originally been an entertainment hall from the looks of the chandelier, had been converted into a soul hold. They hadn't gone to any trouble to make the place welcoming for their catch. Cheap cots and stained futon couches filled the cabin, leaving barely enough room for a few narrow aisles. A circular staircase in one of the back corners was roped off, and the opening to the second level was sealed with weathered boards and plywood. Jenni groaned when she noticed it.

"Time to find door number two?" I asked.

She stormed past me and back outside. Grim's shitty mood was contagious. I felt it pressing in on me too, but I tried to dismiss it as I followed Jenni up to the second-tier deck. Saul and Coreen stood watch below.

Another splintered door revealed an equally disappointing control room. Two bunks were angled against the starboard wall, and an empty desk sat along the port wall. The room was wiped clean. Even the trashcan beside the desk had been emptied.

Jenni swore and kicked the desk chair across the room. I wasn't used to her having outbursts. It made me oddly uncomfortable.

"Hey, we still have Tasha's apartment and that demon boyfriend of hers to check out."

Jenni sighed and twisted her head to the side to pop her neck. "If she took care of the boat, then I'm sure her apartment isn't going to do us any good."

"Then we check out the boyfriend first."

Jenni stormed past me again, but I'd had enough. I caught her arm and made her stop and look at me. "Did I do something to upset you? You're being awfully short with me this morning."

Her brows pinched together as she looked away. "Sorry. I'm just frustrated. Grim threatened to find a new second if I didn't bring back something useful today."

"Grim's a dick," I said, giving her arm a tug. "But he knows no one else would do half as good a job as you. Don't sweat it. Besides, we're going to find something useful. Even if it's just some tranquilizers to slip into his coffee."

Jenni snorted. "I'm sure Ellen would be on board with that plan."

I grinned, wondering if Ellen would be able to keep a straight face while delivering laced coffee. "Come on. Let's pay Tack a visit."

We gathered the hounds and took the harbor travel booth to the one on the far west side of Limbo City, where Morte Avenue met Westwood Road. A series of rundown apartment buildings stretched around the block, far from the heart of the city. This neighborhood belonged mostly to souls who worked at the factory, though I had found a nephilim on this side just last year.

Warren, who was responsible for the Nephilim Guard's weaponry, now lived on the same floor as me at Holly House. I had paid his first six months' rent in exchange for the double-headed axe I now wielded in battle and decapitated minor deities with. In other words, it was totally worth the price.

Tack, the demon lover in question, lived in a building a few down from Warren's old residence. The exterior brick crumbled around rusty balconies. A few had pulled away from the building, drooping hazardously over the sidewalk. Inside was worse. The carpet in the lobby was worn through in places and reeked of urine. An empty vending machine had been turned on its side, and the glass kicked in. The hounds noticed and carefully stepped around the broken pieces.

OUT OF ORDER had been scrawled across both elevators in permanent marker, so we took the stairs. I feared we would find the apartment as abandoned and useless as the yacht but was pleasantly surprised when we stopped on the

third floor. A talk show blared through the wall, and the choking smell of cigarettes seeped around Tack's apartment door.
I pulled a can of angelica mace out of my pocket and shook it
as Saul and Coreen flanked me. Then, for the third time that
morning, Jenni kicked in a locked door.

CHAPTER TEN

"History is a pack of lies
we play on the dead."
—Voltaire

Tack was a hellfire junkie. He couldn't have weighed a hundred pounds, and he seemed more interested in picking at the scabs in the crook of his arm than reacting to our theatrical entrance. Even as the hounds circled him on his ratty, plaid sofa, Tack's eyelids stayed open at half-mast. A pair of webbed wings sagged behind his shoulders, snagging on the couch cushions.

"My papers are good for *least* another week," he slurred around the butt of a cigarette.

A dirty blanket was stapled to the wall above the window in the kitchen, and the small bit of light that slipped through illuminated the smoke and dust particles in the air.

Jenni slowly drew her katana. "When is the last time you spoke with Tasha Henry?"

Tack ignored her and limply reached for a syringe on the coffee table. He didn't even come close. Jenni's blade zipped through the air as she brought it down on his fingers, slicing them off at the knuckles. Blood sprayed over the table and across Tack's shirt as he cradled his hand to his chest. His eyes finally opened all the way, and he took us in with a strangled cry. The cigarette fell from his mouth and onto the floor.

"You can't—you can't… I'm legal," he stammered.

While the laced hellfire was clearly an issue, it wouldn't have usually been corrected so severely. I tried not to cringe away from Jenni as she flicked the blood from her blade, leaving a ragged red line across the dingy carpet.

"Let's try again. When is the last time you spoke with Tasha Henry?"

Tack blinked at her, lost somewhere between his high and the shock of blood loss. "She left me last week. For some asshole that showed up at one of my parties."

"Does this asshole have a name?"

"Why the fuck should I care what his name is?"

Jenni looped her blade in the air. "I can think of at least five reasons off-hand."

Tack swallowed. "Devin. He's with the rebels."

"You don't say," Jenni said dryly. "What's his in to Limbo City?"

"I think he drives a cab. Yeah, that's how he ended up at my party in the first place."

A howl came from the hallway. "You pathetic snitch!"

Coreen snarled as a piece of the front door flew past my face. I ducked as a second piece hurled over my head and bounced off Tack's shoulder.

The demon in the doorway looked familiar, but it took me a minute to peg her as the crazy bitch who'd burned down my apartment last spring. Her eyes were sunken, and her collarbone and elbows pressed sharply through her skin. It didn't take her long to recognize me.

"You," she hissed. Being shriveled and strung out didn't affect her combustion abilities. Her fists flamed to life like giant matchsticks as she launched herself into the room.

The scar on my neck had mostly faded, but I felt it prickle as I remembered how she had pinned me to my kitchen floor and demanded Winston's location, melting my skin and crushing my throat. Demons weren't really known for their rationale. I pointed my can of angelica mace at her and applied it like eighties' hairspray—generously.

Who would have guessed that angelica mace was flammable? The interior wall of Tack's apartment was suddenly engulfed in flames. Some of the mace found its way into the demon hag's face, so at least I'd bought some time. She clawed at her eyes and screamed at me in Latin.

Jenni's eyes migrated from the fire to the window. Then she scowled. We were on the third floor, and coin travel was inactive in the city. This was not going to be a clean getaway.

"We should kill her." Jenni pointed her blade at the flailing fire demon. "She's clearly with the rebels, and she's a hazard to Limbo City."

"If she's with the rebels, I bet she has more information than Tack here."

Jenni ground her teeth. "I'm pretty sure Grim won't be too pleased if we bring her in and she sets fire to the office."

"Is there anyone else you have in mind to beat some good news out of today?"

Sweat popped up along Jenni's brow as the room turned into a furnace. "Damn it, Lana." She marched over and dropped the demon with a swift kick to the knee before positioning her blade over the fiend's heart, both hands firmly around the hilt. "Talk. Now."

The demon laughed. Her eyes were blistered shut from the mace, but I was sure she could feel the tip of Jenni's blade pressing into her breastbone. "I'm a fire demon. These flames do not concern me, but I imagine the heat's already getting to you."

Jenni pressed her sword down just enough to break the skin. "And the hotter I get, the less eager I am to spare you."

"You'll burn to death before I talk."

"If I pass out from the heat, my weight will ensure that you're skewered on my blade."

The demon's grin faltered. Jenni pushed the blade in a bit more.

"Wait! There's a soul in the city making fake passports for the rebels. She does clerical work at the factory. The rebels also pay her to sneak them in and out through the factory sea entrance."

"Is there a rebel base in the city still?"

Her frown deepened. "I wouldn't know. I was demoted after I set fire to the Coexist Complex and got arrested in the raid at Purgatory Lounge." Her face turned toward me accusingly.

The apartment walls were turning black. They shrank in on themselves, and the ceiling groaned in protest, cracking inward from the corners. Smoke stained the air as the fire crept closer, peeling up the carpet along the way. Somewhere in the midst of the chaos, Tack had found time to snatch up the syringe of hellfire. It stuck out of his arm like it had been stabbed there. His fingerless hand lay across his lap, bleeding down his pant leg. The hounds circled me, whimpering a soft warning that our time was growing short.

I backed away from the fire and into the kitchen. "Jenni?"

She ignored me, carrying on with her interrogation, sweat dripping from her nose. "Where was the base before your demotion?"

The demon's teeth chattered, and her shoulders trembled as if she had caught a chill. The room was suffocating, and Jenni's eyes fluttered as she swayed on her feet, her boots brushing against the demon's splayed arms. The movement was enough to give away Jenni's position. The demon's hands flamed to life again, and she grasped Jenni's ankles, melting through the leather of her boots.

Jenni screamed and shoved her blade through the demon's chest, giving it a sharp jerk upward. She stumbled back, pulling her charred legs free with a cry. The fire had completely consumed the interior walls now. Only the window in the kitchen invited us to survive. Coreen stood under it and barked while Saul nudged me in her direction.

Jenni barely had the energy to sheath her katana. She hunched over and rested her arms on her knees, panting through the thickening smoke. "We have two new leads."

"We have one exit." I coughed and wheezed in a painful breath.

Jenni wiped a hand down her face and shook her head. She still looked unsteady. Her hesitance sparked panic in me. Reflection and careful planning was not meant for times like this. I pushed the curtain back and tried to open the kitchen window, but the building had settled around it, and at least two layers of thick, cheap paint sealed it shut.

A crooked card table and a pair of rusty metal chairs sat in the corner of Tack's kitchen. I grabbed one of the chairs and hurled it through the window. The glass shattered, leaving shards like broken teeth around the edges. I pulled a hunting knife from my boot and used the handle to break away the rest of the glass. The smoke funneled out the window, dragging the fire closer to us and quickening my pulse.

I gave the blanket-curtain a tug and pushed it through the window, sticking my head out to see how far it would get us. There was a questionable looking balcony protruding from the apartment beneath Tack's. I didn't have long to worry if it would hold our weight. Coreen leapt past me. She landed hard on the balcony and it wobbled, sprinkling the sidewalk with bits of rusty brick. She quickly jumped over the railing and to the pavement below, barking the all-clear to Saul, who nudged my hip with his muzzle.

Jenni stuck her head out the window beside me and sucked in the clean air. She kicked her legs over the windowsill and shimmied down the blanket, dropping to the balcony soundlessly before catapulting over the railing like a gymnast.

"Show off."

I crawled over the sill and slid down the curtain awkwardly. Just before reaching the balcony, the staples holding the ratty fabric to the apartment wall gave out, one by one. My fingers slipped, and I was rudely deposited on the rusty balcony. A second later, Saul touched down beside me. The spreading fire flashed through the sliding glass door behind us, disappearing from view as the building shucked the balcony with an industrial groan.

Saul and I had just enough time to stand and step over the railing before the balcony crashed to the sidewalk, ending in a mangled mass of rusty limbs curled up like a dead spider.

Fat drops of water splashed down from the sky. Someone had contacted Zibel, the weather god who worked at Bank of Eternity, to put out the fire. It sizzled and hissed in the rain, while ribbons of smoke spiraled up from the charred remains of the building.

Jenni grabbed my arm and pulled me across the street. "If we get out of here fast enough, maybe we can avoid the paperwork."

The hounds trailed us as we stumbled down the street toward the nearest travel booth.

⌒

CHAPTER ELEVEN

'It is the mark of an educated mind to be able to entertain a
thought without accepting it."
—Aristotle

"**W**ho keeps backup shoes in their office?"

"I do." Jenni tossed a pair of black, leather flats at me and turned to dig through a box on the floor of her coat closet. "I also keep a first-aid kit in here somewhere."

Reapers Inc. was quieter now. Ellen informed us on our return that Grim had stepped out for an emergency meeting, more than likely due to the fire I'd accidentally started. But to be fair, the fire demon was just as much to blame. Of course, her being dead would probably leave the brunt of the accusation on me. Maybe Jenni would help soften the blow—though she was short on brownie points lately, too.

Jenni had been promoted to Grim's second-in-command at the same time I'd made captain of the Posy Unit, but unlike me, she'd actually earned her new title. Which was probably why she had the bigger office. Her job description was a bit loftier than mine too, but she had managed to find time to break in her new space.

The heady aroma of temple incense wafted from a brazier hanging above a giant vase of ornamental grass. The smell dueled with the stench of my wet hounds, sprawled out in front of a pair of leather benches. A mammoth of a desk sat in the center of the room, leaving a wide span of empty space between her desk chair and a glass weapons cabinet along the far wall where display lights fell over an impressive collection of knives, katanas, and a few antique weapons, including a Chinese bronze sword.

"Here we are." Jenni tossed a plastic first-aid box onto her desk and slumped down in her chair. She twisted a leg up and rested it over her knee, wincing at the charred leather fused to her ankle.

"You sure you don't want to pay Meng a visit?"

Her face turned to stone. "I'd rather not."

"Yeah, okay." I set the pair of flats down on the desk and knelt in front of her. "Let me help at least."

Jenni rolled up her pant leg while I puzzled over where to begin. There was a tiny zipper running along the backside of the boot. It looked like it was intact. I unzipped it a little at a time, pausing when Jenni hissed or swore. Once that was done, the rest was much easier to peel off.

We'd just started on the second boot when Grim barreled in. He closed the door before stalking across the room and slapping both palms down on Jenni's desk.

"I certainly hope you acquired something useful from this disaster. Cindy Morningstar is not thrilled right now. She's been carrying on and on about this demon suffrage nonsense, and now I imagine she has all the ammunition she needs to stir up the next council meeting."

Grim's eyes were dark, and his hair was sticking out all over the place. He looked like Jack Nicholson. On a bad day. At least he hadn't started breaking things again. Saul sneezed and then whimpered when Grim shot him a disgusted look.

"Rules, Ms. Harvey," he said through gritted teeth.

I cringed. "Sorry. We were in a rush. Didn't have time to drop them off at home."

Jenni groaned as she leaned away from me and peeled off the rest of her boot. She propped her bare feet up on the desk in Grim's face, giving him a full view of her blistered ankles and calves. "We have two new leads. Tasha ran off with some rebel demon by the name of Devin. He's a cab driver in the city. Also, a fire demon—one who was rounded up last spring in the raid at Purgatory Lounge—mentioned that a soul at the factory has been helping rebels infiltrate the city."

Grim straightened and folded his arms. "You get the name of this soul?"

"No. The demon set the building on fire, so we were pressed for time. And then she attacked me." Jenni nodded to her feet. "I had to exterminate her."

I felt better about butting into the conversation now that Jenni had credited the fire solely to the demon. "How did she find her way back on the streets? Shouldn't she have been executed or imprisoned or *something* after the raid?"

Grim snarled at me. "The demon community in Limbo is in upheaval. I would have loved to give the axe to the whole lot we rounded up, but Cindy Morningstar thought that would just fuel the rebels' cause and drive more recruits their way."

"So you just let them go?"

"The ones we didn't have sufficient evidence against were deported, but clearly they're finding their way back into the city."

Jenni nodded. "We'll take care of it—"

"*After* you find Hypnos." Grim's voice shook as he pierced us with his bloodshot eyes. He slapped the desk. "I expect a new mission proposal by the end of the day."

Jenni gave him a weak nod. "Lana really should get back to her harvests. The new reapers haven't been transferred to her team yet."

"I'll have Ellen send transfer orders today. They can start tomorrow. *Just find Hypnos.*" He stormed off without another word, slamming the office door behind him.

I gave Jenni a puzzled look. "Shouldn't finding the rebel base and this traitor soul take priority over a minor deity whose presence isn't entirely necessary?"

Her shoulders sagged, and she rubbed a hand over her eyes. "I don't get paid to understand Grim's reasons. I just do what I'm told."

I tapped my fingers on the first-aid kit and tilted my head at her feet. "You gonna be able to dress those yourself?"

"I'll manage. Just go harvest some souls with Josie. Maybe it will clear the air a little. I've had enough dirty looks for one day."

I gave her a mock salute and left for the afternoon bombing where I'd promised the team I would join them. Prime bonding time, for sure.

CHAPTER TWELVE

*"Don't let your studies
interfere with your education."*
—Henry Rutgers

Josie's persistence was infuriating. Her silent treatment unraveled into short, dismal replies. By the end of the day, I was ready to kick her in the shins to see if I could get more than two words out of her. The emotional beat-down had me doing the math in my head—just to see if the two new Posies might be able to handle the workload if we taught Josie the secret mission handshake. Either way, this guilt trip needed to be over. Now.

My exhaustion flared into anxiety as soon as I clocked out. Bub's first class was tonight. I'd been harboring an uneasy feeling ever since Asmodeus had shown up at the harbor looking for him. I resisted the urge to call and ask where he was and who he was with. There was a naïve hope left in me that once I saw him at the academy, everything would be fine. We'd be just fine. He'd teach class. We'd go have dinner. Then he'd take me back to Tartarus and make up for lost time.

The knot in my stomach grew as I tried to decide on an appropriate outfit. Bub would undoubtedly point me out and request a shining review. Maybe a demonstration. I settled on charcoal slacks and a slinky red blouse. Then I added a pair of black pumps and glossy red lipstick. I left my hair down, letting the dark ringlets graze my jawline. The final look was meant to be half business casual and half come-hither, demon mine.

The rest of the gang was eating pizza when I entered the dining room to fetch a scarf from the coat closet. I raised my eyebrows at Jenni when Josie turned her back, silently requesting if there had been any improvement. Jenni gave me a lopsided frown and shrugged.

"I'm heading to the academy to sit in on Bub's first class. Don't be late, Kevin." I shook my finger at him with a bogus scowl. Kevin's laughter was cut short by a sharp look from Josie. Then I scowled for real. "Try not to have too much fun while I'm gone." I shot Jenni a sympathetic smile and left.

I took the travel booths across town to the academy and made it to Bub's classroom thirty minutes early. He hadn't arrived yet. I shouldn't have been surprised, but I was.

A handful of old writing desks filled the room, staggered up wide, raised platforms that curved around in auditorium fashion. A dusty chalkboard stretched across the wall behind Bub's chair, and a stack of textbooks rested on the corner of his desk. I thumbed through one while I waited.

The reading was lighter than what I had been assigned during my two-week crash course, though there was an extended reading list in the foreword, which I was delighted to see had been written by Jack. At least he was getting some sort of credit for all the work he'd done.

Ten minutes before class, students began trickling in. I made myself useful and handed out the textbooks. I caught a few sideways glances, a few polite nods, genuine greetings from Kevin and Clair. Only one reaper was brave enough to openly sneer at me. She was a skinny thing, with a flirty pony-tail tied off to one side and draped over her shoulder. She chomped loudly on a wad of chewing gum as she gave me an unimpressed once-over and snatched a book out of my hand. I returned the look halfheartedly.

Most of the class arrived before Bub finally decided to show. My relief was hard to suppress—and so was my annoy-ance. I gave him a forced smile and took a seat at an empty desk in the front row.

Bub gave me a curt nod before scrawling his name across the chalkboard in all caps. On the last letter, he dug his fin-gernails into the board, echoing a shocking screech across the room. He spun around and assessed the class, immediately pointing out a young reaper cringing away from the sound.

"You," he snapped, pointing his finger. "Out of my class-room."

"W-what?" The guy trembled and knocked his textbook to the floor.

"If you can't handle nails on a chalkboard, then you won't make it past week two in this class. Save us both the trouble and drop out now."

The rejected reaper kept his eyes on the floor as he turned in his textbook and left. The rest of the students shrank in their seats, anticipating the next cut. All except for Miss

Bubblegum Ponytail. She stared right at Bub, smiling, almost daring him to try her.

Bub put down the chalk and picked up a textbook. He waved it in the air. "Assignment number one: read the first three chapters and write a two-page summary, including an explanation for why you think this class is critical to your current or future career path."

The brave little reaper shot her hand into the air, asking her question before Bub had the chance to call on her. "Don't you think *you* should be answering why this class is critical? Why what you have to teach us holds more clout than what we'd learn in any other class?"

Bub clicked his tongue. "And you are?"

"Lacey Irman."

"Well, Ms. Irman, I don't fancy groveling. Either you want to know how to defend yourself against demons, or you don't. If you do, then I suggest you keep your pretty little mouth shut. I'll be teaching this class my way. I was hired for the job, after all."

"All right then, professor B." She folded her legs under her desk and grinned as if he'd just complimented her rather than told her to shut her face.

"One last thing," Bub said, raising his voice for the whole class to hear. "Ms. Harvey will be substituting for me next Monday. You'll be turning your essays over to her. Class dismissed."

I stayed in my seat, hands clenched into fists in my lap as the students filtered out of the room. I pressed my lips together and stared at the ceiling, waiting to be alone with Bub so I could unleash my wrath.

When the door closed, I zeroed in on him. "Did you seriously announce that I'm going to substitute for your class without even running it by me first?"

Bub sat on the edge of his desk and wet his lips, refusing to look at me. "I'm rather busy with orders from the Hell Committee right now."

"How exactly are you getting orders from them when you're not even going to the meetings?"

His head jerked up, and he glared at me.

"Asmodeus stopped by the harbor looking for you. I'm guessing he wasn't supposed to let that particular cat out of the bag."

"Lana, it's not what you think—"

"What do I think? Tell me. I'm curious." I stood and walked toward his desk, leaning on the opposite side to mirror him.

"My orders kept me from the last meeting. Our rebel spies are proving fruitless now that their last known general is dead." His brow dropped into a condemning line.

I sniffed. "Are you reprimanding me for doing my job?"

"Technically, your job is to harvest souls."

"And to substitute for your class, apparently." I shook my head. "I have my own set of orders. From the Afterlife Council."

Bub's scowl softened to something that crossed between remorse and annoyance. "They still have you on retainer? But you've eliminated Caim. What more do they want from you?"

"Oh, yes, let me spell out all the council secrets I've been forbidden to share. I don't really need my head anyway, right?"

"Lana, this is serious. I'm worried about your safety." Bub stepped in closer and dropped his voice.

"Oh, so your worry trumps orders from the council now? What about my worry? Does that entitle me to the Hell Committee's secrets?"

Bub turned away from me with a growl. He paced a few steps and then turned around, stalking back toward me with his finger in the air. "You're right. Of course you are. We can't share our secrets, no matter how much we want to protect each other. Politics and"—he waved his hand between us—"this do not mix well." He sighed and looked away. "I'm sorry, love. I truly am."

I thought winning the argument would have made me feel better. But I only felt worse. Bub looked broken, and I hated it. But I couldn't do any more about it than he could.

I ran a hand down his arm and turned him into me, linking my fingers behind his neck as I pressed my forehead to his. "Can we forget all of this bullshit for tonight and just enjoy each other? It's been too long."

Bub tucked a curl behind my ear. "It has."

"Tartarus?"

He tensed. "Do you mind if we stay at your place tonight?"

I'd been looking forward to the privacy of his summer home. The thought of Josie, Kevin, and Jenni listening to us through the walls was a total mood killer. "I have a better idea."

We left and took the academy travel booth to the one at the end of Ghost Alley, catty-corner from a dive Thai restaurant that Josie and I frequented—or used to frequent. Then we grabbed some takeout and hopped back in the travel booth, taking it to the harbor. It was the perfect time to break in the new cabin.

We hardly spoke the rest of the evening, keeping our secrets on the tips of our tongues where they were safe. The Thai food was forgotten on the desk once I fired up the oil lamps and Bub caught sight of the pristine, white bed. It was like a blank page, begging us to write ourselves all over it. And we did.

I fell asleep tangled in Bub's arms, my anger and guilt muted by bliss, the tightness in my chest releasing naively.

A few hours later, I woke to the ring of Bub's cellphone. He uncoiled himself from around my waist and slipped out of bed, while I pretended to sleep. It was dark outside, probably nearing midnight. The oil lamps had dimmed, casting the room in sallow light.

Bub answered on the second ring. "What?" he whispered.

I couldn't make out the other end of the conversation— just an angry, feminine garble that was more than likely Cindy Morningstar. Bub's shoulders contracted as if he had been struck through the receiver.

"Fine. I'm leaving now." He rubbed his free hand down his thigh nervously. "Of course not. I haven't told a soul." His spine straightened, and he shivered. "I understand."

I closed my eyes as he hung up and glanced over his shoulder. He was getting ready to bail on me. I was too tired and too hurt to go through the motions with him again. I knew it wasn't his fault, but that didn't make it suck any less.

Bub leaned over until I felt his breath on my neck, where he laid a gentle kiss. "I'm so sorry," he whispered.

I listened to him move around the cabin, quickly throwing on his clothes. A second later, the cabin door closed behind him.

CHAPTER THIRTEEN

I stayed on the ship overnight, having too much pride to make the walk of shame back to Holly House. I didn't sleep, though. Instead, my mind picked at the secrets I was keeping, questioning their merit. Then I pondered Bub's secrets. Then I puzzled over Grim's anxiety and whatever it was he was clearly not sharing.

Around five in the morning, Jenni called. "Where are you?" she asked gruffly.

"Good morning to you, too."

"You better have your shit together. We have a new mission, so you're not going to have much time to break in your new unit members."

"I'll have Josie show them the ropes." I grimaced. "This should go over well."

"Make it snappy, Harvey. I've got an interview with Dave this afternoon, and I have souls to tend to." She hung up without a goodbye.

I crawled out of bed and took a shower in the tiny bathroom tucked into the corner of my new cabin. Josie or Kevin had sorted my clothing out of the closet of the old cabin and left it in a box on the desk. I rummaged through it until I found a pair of jeans and a green tank top. I dressed quickly. Then I threw on my work robe and left for Reapers Inc.

"Oh, honey." Ellen hopped up from her desk the second she saw me. "Let me get you a coffee. You look like you could use one."

"That obvious?" I snatched the harvest list off her desk as she ducked into the break room.

"I sure hope it was worth it," she said, poking her head around the corner as she shook a bottle of creamer. "Jenni looked like she was going to murder kittens when she left."

"Joy." I scanned over the day's harvests and began filling out the dockets. The two new reapers went a long way in lightening the burden of my absence, but I was still going to have hell to pay with Josie. There was no way to get around her suspicions this morning.

Ellen returned to her desk and handed me a travel mug. "At least Grim took the day off, so I don't have to deal with his destructo theatrics. Thought I was going to have to trade my chocolate for Xanax." She adjusted the polka-dotted scarf around her neck and hummed.

I offered her a weak smile.

"Oh! And I called a few decorators about your office. I scheduled meetings for you with three of them, but they're a few weeks out. Busy people, decorators."

"You're the best." I raised the mug of coffee at her in thanks before heading out and back to the harbor.

It was a little early yet, but the new reapers were waiting for me near the ship. It was a promising sight and made me feel both better about and guilty for having to skip out on their first day on the job.

Molly Driver was five foot nothing in her stiletto ankle boots. She had a long braid that fell over her shoulder and snaked its way between her breasts. The look would have been more severe if not for her bright green, anime eyes. She smiled at me and stuck out her hand. I shook it with a grin.

"Good morning."

"Yes, very good morning," she said breathlessly. Even as a fourth-generation reaper, there wasn't a scrap of superiority about her. I wanted to like her right away.

Tyler Ives' face and handshake were more reserved, but at least he was polite. "Thank you for the opportunity to prove my worth," he said firmly, militantly. Like he wanted to tack *sir* on at the end. He was tall, and his hair was buzzed short, reminding me of Craig Hogan. A worm of anxiety swirled in my stomach.

I tried not to be too obvious as I wiped my hand down the side of my robe. "The rest of the team should be here soon. After introductions, I'll pass out soul dockets and set you up with your shadows for the day."

Molly blinked her big eyes at me. "*You're* not shadowing us?"

"I have an appointment this morning, but I promise you'll be well taken care of." I changed the subject before she started asking questions I couldn't answer. "I hear your first pick was the Mother Goose Unit."

Molly blushed. "Yes, I enjoy interacting with children when I have the chance."

"Then you probably know of Arden Faraji."

She nodded eagerly.

"He takes care of most of our harvests involving children. So, I thought you'd enjoy working with him today." I set my coffee down on top of a dock post and flipped through the harvest list before turning to Tyler. "You'll be going with Josie Galla and my apprentice Kevin Kraus. Kevin began under Coreen Bendura too, so you have some common ground. The three of you will be covering a series of post-war zones today. Nothing too stressful, just time-consuming."

Tyler's reserve cracked for a split second as a small frown creased his mouth, but he ducked his head in a sharp nod of acceptance.

A bellow ripped through the air just before Saul plowed me down, pinning me to the dock with his rough paws so he could lap up the side of my face. Coreen wasn't far behind, and Josie and Kevin followed.

"Hey." Kevin waved a hand at the new reapers.

The rest of the team joined us a moment later. Once we were all gathered, I got down to business, passing out dockets and reiterating the game plan for the day.

Josie's steely gray eyes drilled through me, but she didn't say a word. Her jaw tensed as I dismissed everyone. I made it back to my cabin before I realized she was following me.

"You're supposed to be shadowing Tyler." I peeled off my robe and tossed it onto the bed.

Josie leaned against the doorframe and folded her arms. "I sent him ahead with Kevin and the hounds." She glanced around the cabin, taking in the rumpled sheets and the boxes of takeout on the desk. "You have a sleepover with Bub? Or is that top-secret information, too?"

I slumped on the edge of the bed and put my head in my hands. "Yeah, I had a sleepover with Bub. And before you ask, yes, I'm working with Jenni today. I honestly have no idea what we're doing, and I honestly wish you were coming with us. Jenni tried to get approval from Grim, but he was worried about leaving the unit understaffed."

Her eyes quit scanning the room and landed on me. "I can't help but feel left in the dust. You get that, right?" Her forehead crinkled. "A couple years ago, Jenni would have laughed at the notion of choosing you over me for a special mission."

I frowned but nodded in agreement.

Josie unfolded her arms and held her hands out. "I don't know how else to feel about this or what to do about it. All I know is that I want my best friend back. I made Kevin go shopping with me yesterday."

"Really?"

Her eyes darkened. "Yeah. It wasn't pretty."

"Sorry." I pressed my lips together.

"So, I'm thinking I'll forgive you for keeping secrets and avoiding me—but only if you go to Athena's with me after work today."

"Deal."

Josie gave me a guarded smile. "Okay. I'm going to catch up to the boys and make sure they're playing nice."

After she'd left, I made my way back to Reapers Inc., where I pillaged through my desk and geared up with all the spare holy water and angelica mace I had on hand. Whatever we were doing today, I wanted to be ready. Jenni walked in as I tucked a pair of throwing knives down into my boots.

"We're just doing surveillance today. You probably won't need all of that." She was dressed down in jeans and a tee shirt with a tattered messenger bag strapped across her chest.

I shrugged. "Better safe than dead."

I followed Jenni down the hall, pausing to wave goodbye to Ellen. Once we were closed up in the elevator, I nudged Jenni with my shoulder. "I'm going shopping with Josie after work today."

Jenni snorted. "She skipped the gym and had coffee with me this morning."

"Guess we're out of the doghouse."

The elevator doors pinged open on the festive lobby. We made our way outside, and Jenni grabbed my arm, steering me east down Council Street, away from the travel booth on Tombstone Drive that we normally took.

"Too many eyes," she said. "And it's not that far of a walk to the park."

"The park?"

"I called and got Devin's schedule. He's supposed to pick up a fare at the factory around eight. If that's where the rebels are getting in, we might get lucky today."

"So, we're going to watch from the park. And then what? Jump out in traffic to stop him?"

Jenni rolled her eyes. "We'll confirm whether or not he's transporting a known rebel and report back to Grim."

A full city block sat between the park and the factory. It was half parking lot and half picnic seating for employee breaks. The northeast corner of the park was lined with thick hedges and shaded by old oak trees. We found a secluded bench with a decent view of the factory and made ourselves comfortable. It would have looked less suspicious if we'd brought coffee, but we were far enough away to go unnoticed.

It seemed odd that a cab would be picking someone up from the factory at this hour. The Fates' employees would have just clocked in. A visiting deity seemed more reasonable. But why wouldn't a visiting deity schedule a drop-off, too?

The question probably hadn't even occurred to Skipper, the owner of Hop, Skip, and Jump Taxi Service. He was lucky to still be in business. The travel booths were quicker and cheaper. Only tourists cared to take in the city from the backseat of a cab anymore.

Jenni pulled a small pair of binoculars out of her bag and peeked through them as she recapped everything she'd learned from her chat with Skipper. He had hired Devin shortly after the Nephilim Guard snatched up his best employee. He wasn't fond of the guy, but his only other driver was a tree spirit, and she wasn't very reliable. He was considering selling his business and going to work for Cern, the horned god who ran Bank of Eternity. Skipper was small for a troll, but he was fierce and proud. And he had a natural talent for guarding things.

Just after eight, Devin's cab pulled up in front of the factory. Jenni lifted her binoculars and clicked a button on the side. She pressed the button again as Devin stepped out of the cab. He wasn't especially obvious for a demon, lacking horns and a tail. His khakis were wrinkled, and he was in desperate need of a haircut. The only thing remotely demonic about him was the sharp point of his beakish nose. He ran around to the other side of the car, touching the brim of his golf cap as he opened the back door for a hooded figure that emerged from around the side of the factory.

"No way." Jenni pressed a different button, and the lenses rotated, adjusting the zoom and focus. She swallowed and silently passed the binoculars to me. "Is that who I think it is?"

I caught just a glimpse before the car door closed. "Miranda."

Jenni nodded.

"So. Back to the office?" I handed the binoculars to her, but she pushed them away.

"Give me one of your knives."

"What?"

"Quick." She slapped my leg. I dug a knife out of my boot, and she grabbed it, springing to her feet.

The cab was pulling away from the curb, heading west toward Destiny Avenue. Jenni ducked low along the hedges, trying to stay out of sight as the flora thinned on the opposite side of the park. I stumbled along after her, taking cover behind trees and picnic tables, wondering exactly when her brain had fallen out. Badass or not, bringing a knife to a car fight was monumentally stupid. It all felt very double-oh-seven gone wrong.

Jenni was still a good distance away from the road when the cab rolled by. Whatever she had planned, the window of opportunity looked pretty well closed to me. Apparently not. She dropped to one knee and launched the knife, torpedoing it into the front driver's side tire. The rubber split with a sharp pop, and the cab came to a wobbling stop along the shoulder.

Jenni moved quickly, doing her best to stay hidden as she closed in. A flat tire wasn't especially suspect—but a flat tire with a knife sticking out of it would definitely raise a red flag. I hurried after her, holding my breath as the seconds stretched by.

Devin's door opened. His boots crunched along the sparse gravel that lined the road. He yanked off his cap and tossed it back into the taxi, mouthing a few choice words before slamming the door. When his eyes fell on the hilt of the knife, they swelled with panic.

"Go! Go! Go!" He pounded his fist on the side of the car.

The passenger door opened, and Miranda took off, running back toward the factory. Jenni gave up seeking cover and tore after her.

Devin reached for his door and then glanced back at the blown tire. He kicked the car with a growl before taking off down the road in the opposite direction as Jenni and Miranda. By then, I had reached the road. My breath was short, but I was quiet as I approached. I tapped Devin on the shoulder, and when he spun around, he got a face full of angelica mace.

While Devin writhed on the ground, trying to claw out his eyes, I called the Nephilim Guard and gave them our location. I wasn't equipped to detain or haul in villains. Jenni wasn't either, I noted as she led Miranda back toward the cab by the hood of her robe. Miranda wrenched herself free, shedding the robe with a shriek.

Jenni threw a punch as if she expected it to go right through Miranda's face and out the back of her skull. It almost sounded like it had. Miranda's lip exploded. She sucked in a ragged, bloody breath and jerked her knee up, but Jenni blocked it just shy of her kidney before delivering an unforgiving elbow strike to Miranda's temple. Miranda crumpled into an unconscious heap on the ground.

I nudged her with the toe of my boot. "Guess I missed Grim giving you a license to kill."

Jenni squatted down and wiped off her knuckles on Miranda's sleeve. "She's not dead. Not yet, anyway."

The Nephilim Guard didn't take long to arrive. Two winged guards climbed out of a black SUV and cuffed Devin and Miranda before shepherding them into the backseat. Another guard saluted Jenni and me before opening a door and offering us a ride back to the office. I crawled inside ahead of Jenni, not giving her a chance to say no. I'd just sprinted across the entire length of the city park.

Miranda came to during the short ride to Reapers Inc. She took in the interior of the SUV and her features pinched together, making her look like a possum. "Congratulations on murdering our beloved general, Jenni. I hear it was a gory affair. If you weren't such an obedient cunt, we probably would have recruited you by now."

Jenni looked amused. "Our? We? Such camaraderie. Tell me, if you're so well connected with the rebels, why didn't we see you among the nude hell raisers on Caim's ship? Didn't you get an invitation to the nightmare orgy?"

Miranda ignored her, flashing her bloody grin at me with a frosty laugh. "You're not off the hook either, Lana. Don't matter that you got passed over for the big promotion. We see your fingers pulling strings. We remember your sins. Seth's not done with you yet."

Jenni ran her hands over the leather seat and glanced down in the floorboard. "I'm sure there's *something* in here we can use as a gag."

One of the guards chuckled. "I'll sacrifice my socks if need be."

Miranda's nose crinkled, and she turned away from us, looking out the window past Devin, whose eyes were nearly swollen shut. He hadn't said a word, just curled himself into the corner of the SUV and rested his head against the window.

Miranda didn't look quite so smug once we pulled into the parking garage of Reapers Inc. Her eyes dilated, and her breath grew labored as we parked. A dozen more guards waited near the elevators, ready to stave off any last-minute escape efforts.

Everyone piled out of the SUV and crammed into an elevator. It was a tight fit, even though the guards all folded their wings tightly against their backs. The silence felt heavier with so many bodies, and the climb to the seventy-fifth floor took longer than ever. When we arrived, Miranda was practically hyperventilating.

"You're wasting your time," she rasped. "I'm no traitor. You won't get me to talk." She thrashed between the two guards flanking her.

Jenni snorted. "Well, you're right about one thing. You've definitely wasted our time."

The elevator opened and Grim stood waiting in front of Ellen's desk, his hands folded behind his back. Miranda's legs went out from under her, and the guards grunted as they bore her full weight.

"Please," she wailed, shaking her head as they dragged her forward.

Santos Consuelo, the captain of the Lost Souls Unit that Miranda had been on up until her disappearance, stepped out of his office to see the commotion. Sorrow creased his face as if he wanted to step forward and vouch for her, but he knew nothing good would come of it.

Miranda's pleading only grew more desperate until the guards stopped her in front of Grim. An eerie silence fell over the room. The whites of Grim's eyes filled with black like a giant squid had just inked inside his skull.

The energy that swirled around the room was sickeningly familiar. I suddenly felt like an addict, panicking at the nearness of my kryptonite. Everyone froze, and it took me a minute to realize that it wasn't from fear. It was Grim's doing.

Time stood still as he reached forward, sinking his hand inside Miranda's chest. An orange glow filled her, bubbling forth like a lava eruption, draining her essence. Her skin paled and became translucent. When Grim pulled out his hand, Miranda collapsed in on herself like a hot air balloon until she disappeared with an anticlimactic pop. Bits of soul matter scattered into the air, evaporating like mist.

The whites of Grim's eyes resurfaced, and I realized he had been looking at me the entire time. I expected him to be surprised, but the cold, vulturine look he gave me sent a film of sweat over my body. I tried to swallow, but my throat refused to cooperate.

Devin, the demon cab driver, looked more agitated and defiant now that he stood alone in the circle of armored guards. Before, he had been content to melt into the background and let Miranda have center stage. But now his buffer was gone. Not that he remembered she had been there in the first place.

"So," Santos said, his sadness forgotten. "You believe this demon has ties to the rebels?"

"I do." Grim nodded once, never taking his eyes from me. "Take him away," he ordered the guards. *To the thirty-seventh floor*, I silently added.

Jenni cleared her throat and turned to Grim, trying to cut off his line of sight to me, not realizing the look on his face was more blame than credit. "Orders?"

Grim's gaze slowly shifted from me to Jenni, and then back to me. "Resume your regular schedules, but report to me first thing tomorrow morning. I'm sure I'll have made some progress with the demon by then."

Jenni scowled, and it occurred to me that she had brought in Miranda, not Devin. I had taken him down. The memory of Miranda's capture had just been zapped out of everyone's mind. The weight of Jenni's resentment smacked me with guilt, even though I had nothing to do with it. She spared me a curt nod before disappearing down the hallway toward her office.

With Ellen away for lunch, once the guards hauled Devin away, I was left alone in the lobby with Grim. Neither of us had moved. His eyes stayed trained on me with contempt as he adjusted his cufflinks. Then he bowed deeply and with flair, like a stage magician. Like Miranda's death had been some extravagant trick, and I'd been the only witness.

CHAPTER FOURTEEN

"The only true wisdom
is in knowing you know nothing."
—*Socrates*

I had plenty of legitimate reasons to skip out on going back to work. But more than anything, I needed the distraction. Any downtime I allowed myself would be spent envisioning what Grim was doing to the demon cab driver on the thirty-seventh floor. What he could be doing to *me* on the thirty-seventh floor. He had looked entirely too comfortable pulling the plug on Miranda, which made me wonder if I had more dubious things to fret over than the floor of horrors at Reapers Inc.

On top of my paranoia was a mountain of questions I wasn't entirely sure I was prepared to have answers for. Did Grim know about Craig Hogan? And if he did, why hadn't he said anything? Had Grim undone anyone else? Did I overlook it, or had it occurred before my time? Or maybe I just didn't know the unexisted in question. I wasn't sure I'd ever have the balls to outright ask Grim. I was better off pretending that Miranda had never existed at all. Maybe Grim would keep pretending that Craig had never been, too.

My pulse was dancing when I reached the harbor. The dock was quiet. The soft hiss of the waves and the soul mist spraying up along the coast did little to calm my nerves. It wasn't long before Josie, Kevin, and Tyler made a pit stop to drop off a lot of souls. I spent the rest of the day shadowing Tyler and doing captainish things as I tried to forget the morning.

After work, my anxiety flared up again. The shopping expedition with Josie didn't go as far as I had hoped in refreshing our friendship. I was distracted, and I was pretty sure she could tell. We wandered around Athena's Boutique, skimming through the new winter line and ending up in the shoe department where all the summer footwear had been marked down. A halfhearted debate over whether or not wedges counted as platforms ended with us both shrugging before heading back to Holly House.

Wednesday morning came too soon. I wasn't ready to see Grim again. The dread that had seeped into me after the Miranda incident hadn't let go. I stopped by the office just long enough to grab my harvest list from Ellen. After the unit meeting, I skipped the travel booths and took the long way back to the office, walking the five blocks from the harbor as if I might somehow convince my heart that it was racing from the workout—and not because I was disregarding all sense of self-preservation.

As the elevator doors opened on the seventy-fifth floor, Jenni barged in and pressed the button for the lobby. "Time to go, Harvey. I've got our new orders."

There was a tinge of smugness in her voice, like she expected me to be put out that Grim hadn't requested an audience with me. I didn't correct her, not wanting to answer the questions it would have spawned.

"Where to?" I asked, trying to contain the bubbling relief that filled me.

"The rebel base in Limbo." She adjusted the chopsticks in her hair and tightened the strap of her katana sheath across her chest. "Where's your axe? Do we need to stop by the condo and pick it up?"

"Don't you think that might draw too much attention while we're in the city? I have knives, holy water, and angelica mace. I've even got throwing stars." I lifted my work robe to show her the crystal-tipped set strapped around my thigh. They had been a gift from Bub during my demon defense training. My heart dipped at the thought of him.

"Whatever." Jenni exited the elevator ahead of me, leading the way out the front door. I was a little more hesitant, scoping out the sidewalk for reporters.

"Come on." Jenni waved me along. "We're safe, for now. I gave Dave an interview yesterday, remember?" She fished a copy of *Limbo Weekly* out of a deep pocket in her robe and slapped it into my hand.

The cover of the magazine was a full-on glamor shot of Jenni, posing with her katana drawn and angled to strike. I smothered a laugh. Dave definitely knew how to guarantee future interviews. While other reporters shredded reputations and burned bridges, he painted his prospects up like saints, to the point that most of them came begging for second and third sit-downs. Talk about job security.

Dave had interviewed several people for the article, mixing up our questions so that it almost seemed like he'd gathered us all together in a secret meeting. Every other journalist in the city was surely fuming by now. Jenni was right. Dave's story would stale the whole Caim fiasco, leaving us to work in peace.

Even though we were reporter-free this morning, Jenni didn't let many mission details slip until we had moseyed off onto a quieter sidewalk. I'd expected the base to be in a rundown apartment like Tack's, but we ended up venturing past the more questionable neighborhoods in Limbo toward the southwestern edge of the island where a small crust of trees tapered off into a beach.

The beaches of Limbo City were not made to be enjoyed with bikinis and mojitos. The sands were rough and rocky, and angry ledges jutted out into the sea. Much farther out, an artificial reef of twisted metal gleamed beneath the waves, warning off illegal vessels. Winged rebels could still fly over the barrier and infiltrate the city, but the Nephilim Guard kept a closer eye on the sea these days. The reef was far enough away to allow plenty of time for a defense brigade to be assembled.

Where the trees began to thin near the shore, three narrow buildings huddled together before a stretch of broken sidewalk. A few decades ago, the place had been a summer resort—a hopeless business venture of Neptune's bored wife, Salacia. The lack of dolphins depressed her, and if that hadn't, the lack of customers would've eventually. No one wanted to sunbathe on gravel or swim in a sea of zombified souls.

Jenni pointed through the trees, and I followed her around to the backside of the first building where a cluster of rusty dumpsters was being assailed by weeds and vines. She hefted herself up on one and peered through a darkened window.

"Check the next building. The dust on the floor is so thick, we should be able to see footprints in it. Let's have something to go on before we make a scene breaking into the place." She hopped down and wove her way through the trees toward the farthest building.

The dumpsters behind the second building were in worse shape than the first. At least, that's what I was prepared to tell Jenni when she complained about the ruckus I made as I climbed on top of them. A rumble from inside froze me in place, just beneath the ledge of the dusty window.

Muffled voices grew louder until I was sure I'd been sniffed out. Sweat trickled down my spine, but I refused to move. The voices were denser now, and I caught the tail end of an argument.

"We can't trust him. As long as he's in good standing with the council, he could be playing either side."

"I thought you said we needed spies," a feminine voice countered.

"Spies we plant *ourselves*. Not convenient enemies that dangle before us like bait."

"But hasn't he proven himself enough? We have Hypnos, don't we?"

"Ha! Hypnos. What good is a sleeping god? His absence was hardly noticed by the factory, and it was shadowed by those bloody reapers' victory over us when they slew Caim."

"True, but it *is* driving Grim mad. He's been reckless lately. He's sure to misstep soon."

"Hmmm. We'll grant him access to the mobile base for now. His loyalties still need testing."

The voices faded off, but I stayed put, straining to hear through the window.

"Lana?" Jenni tapped my foot. I hadn't heard her approach.

"This is the one," I whispered. "And the bastard who abducted Hypnos is with them."

"Good." Jenni unsheathed her katana.

"We don't know how many we're up against."

"There won't be any when we're done."

She had lost her mind. Half the rebel forces could be hiding out in there. It wasn't like Jenni to rush into things. She and Josie shared an OCD love of over-planning the piss out of everything. Grim's threats were really weighing on her, and he wasn't the only one being reckless lately.

I ground my teeth and fetched a knife from my boot before palming a can of angelica mace and hopping off the dumpster.

We stepped lightly on the gravel path leading up to the back entrance. Jenni tested one of the double doors, and then the other. Her shoulders bunched as it creaked open. She moved to wave me in, but then the courtesy washed from her face, and she darted in first.

I never pictured myself as a threat to Jenni Fang. She always seemed so out of my league. It made me wonder what Grim had said about me behind closed doors. Did he use me as a threat? The change in Jenni couldn't all be about the Miranda stunt. Was Grim trying to drive a wedge between us? And to what end?

The inside of the building was dark and humid. Old wiring buzzed in the walls, and the smell of mold was suffocating. I tucked my face into the crook of my arm to stifle a cough and nearly tripped on the first step of a staircase. Even in the dark, I caught the glare Jenni shot me.

A streak of light filtered in through a grimy window on the first landing, positioned halfway before the second floor. It was just enough to help us detect the rotten spots in the stairs as we ascended.

Empty guest rooms stretched down every hall. The quiet was eerie, and I began to wonder if the rebels I'd overhead hadn't left through the front door before we came in. But then we reached the fifth and final floor.

Light chatter hummed from the end of the hallway adjacent to the stairs. It was the kind of quiet, indistinguishable noise I heard at funerals all the time. Nothing like the uproar on Caim's ship. Even though these rebels sounded more tame and rational, my stomach tightened, and a cold sweat spread over me. It was unnerving to think that this crowd of calm, casual rebels was out there wandering the streets of Limbo, plotting to destroy us all.

The floor creaked beneath us as we came off the stairs.

"Quiet," someone hissed.

Jenni grabbed my arm and pulled me around the corner. We wedged ourselves into a dark cubbyhole that looked like it had once housed a vending machine. Then we held our breaths and waited.

The silence stretched on forever, and then slowly, the chatter resumed. I couldn't make out words, but there were at least ten rebels from the variety of range in the voices.

When the conversation's volume reached its former decibel, Jenni's shoulder sagged against mine. She let out a slow breath and peeked around the corner, bringing her katana up just in time to block a lumbering blow from a mace.

The weapon looked like something only a giant could wield—an impossibly stealthy giant, from the silent approach. It was as thick around as my thigh, with a long, nasty ball of spurs that sparked against Jenni's sword. She cowered under the impact, and I suddenly felt like a moron for not bringing my axe. I readied my can of angelica mace and dug deep to find the courage needed to leap under Jenni's waning blade and into the hallway.

"Ha!" I spun around and pointed my can up in the general direction I expected to find a face, but there was no one there. The mace was moving on its own. I didn't have enough time to be stunned. The tail end of the thing arched around and cracked me across the stomach, dropping me to the floor. Thankfully, the spikey end was still preoccupied with Jenni.

"Use your spray! Use the goddamn holy water! Use something," she shrieked, swiping her blade around to block another crippling blow.

I wheezed in a painful breath and wondered how many of my ribs were still intact. Miraculously, the angelica mace was still in my hand. I pointed it at the enchanted weapon and sprayed out half the can, fogging up the hallway.

"Stop!" Jenni coughed into her arm in between blows. "It's not working. Try something else."

I pressed a hand to the wall behind me and pulled myself up. An open door farther down the hall drew my attention, and I pointed it out to Jenni.

She caught my meaning and backed into the room. As the mace came in for its next strike, she rolled under the blow, right back into the hall. I pulled the door closed behind her. We both jumped as the spiked head of the mace slammed against the door. A few barbs wedged their way through the wood.

I blanched at it wide-eyed. "We're so made."

The door rattled on its hinges as the mace splintered into it again.

Jenni tore off down the hall. "Come on," she shouted over her shoulder. "If that's the best they've got, I'm sure we'll manage."

"Define manage." I dug a knife out of my boot and trailed after her.

The battle with the magical mace hadn't lasted long, but it had been noisy. The conference room was nearly empty. Only three rebels remained—well, two and a half. One was making its way out of a window, digging her clawed feet into the brick as it scaled the building.

The two trapped demons turned and howled at us. One had a halo of horns cupped in toward a concaved skull. Electricity sparked between his horn tips as his face uncurled a viper tongue. The other demon almost looked human, save for a long rat tail that thrashed aggressively around his ankles, snapping against the floor like a whip.

Jenni lifted her sword. "You want to check the roof while I question these two?"

"And by question, do you mean disembowel?"

"Whatever works."

I backed out of the room and did a quick search of the fifth floor until I found the stairs leading to the rooftop. My toenails just weren't equipped for climbing brick walls. Some of the demons were undoubtedly long gone by now, but I was going to get a good look at all the ones I could. Just in case they stayed in the city. That way, I'd be able to identify them before they tried to eat my face off. Maybe Grim would get a sketch artist and see about slapping their likenesses on milk cartons or something.

The door to the roof opened loudly, clanging against its metal frame as the wind wrenched it out of my hand. The fleeing demon from the window clung to the corner of the roof and hissed at me. She posed on all fours, curling her fingers and talony toes over the ledge. The wind ripped at her greasy hair, pulling it back from her face to reveal a too wide mouth full of needle-sharp teeth. She tilted her head to one side, assessing me with round, frightened eyes. Apparently, she hadn't looked in a mirror lately.

I pointed my knife and can of angelica mace at her. "Stay."

The dog command seemed to snap her out of it, shifting her fear into annoyed rage. She hissed at me again as the muscles along her naked back tensed and swelled. Then she was airborne, sprawling across the gap between the buildings like a giant fucking frog. A winged demon squawked out a triumphant laugh and scooped her up under the arms, taking flight over the beach and sea.

Between the shore and the shadow of the defense reef, a yacht bobbed in the waves. It was impossible, but there it was. The demons retreated to it.

"Let's fly, fly boy." A sultry voice from the opposite building rendered me useless.

I knew that pet name. The world went slo-mo as I turned around. It couldn't be him. I was seeing things. I took a step closer, but then he turned. Our eyes locked, and I couldn't find my next breath. I couldn't move. I couldn't blink.

Bub's shoulders stiffened, but he didn't cower. He was dressed in the black military getup he usually wore during a mission. It looked all wrong on him today, exuding an arrogant and menacing air about him. I didn't see the regret that I longed for in his expression.

A rebel demon stood on the rooftop beside him. She was scaly and nude. Her slender fingers clamped down on his shoulder, and I silently vowed to break every single one of them. Twice. Bub turned to look the harlot over with a cunning grin. Then he wrapped an arm around her waist and took flight, dipping down to the yacht waiting off the shore.

I swallowed and remembered to breathe through the acid pooling in my chest. I didn't have time to sort through my inner carnage just yet.

"Any strays up here?" Jenni shouted as she burst through the door behind me.

I shook my head stiffly, not trusting my voice.

She sheathed her blade and slung the case over her shoulder before joining me on the ledge of the roof and following my line of sight to the yacht in the distance. The demons on deck were too far away to recognize now.

The wind sent ripples across the surface of the sea and carried a grating victory cheer with it over the water to us. It ripped the fight right out of me. A sinkhole bubbled open beneath the small boat, and the cheers faded beneath the waves.

Jenni's brows scrunched together. "Let's report back to Grim."

CHAPTER FIFTEEN

I put on my best charade face for the report session with Grim, but it dissolved as soon as I was off the clock. I felt dead inside.

Nothing lasts forever. I knew that. But I'd gotten better at forgetting it lately thanks to the sweet nothings Bub was always whispering in my ear. Sweet nothings that I replayed in my mind and berated myself for getting lost in. Every drop of elation that had trickled through me in the short months we'd been together now felt like a slow-working poison finally taking its toll. My pride was bruised, but it was nothing compared to the gaping wound in my chest.

I took the travel booths to Holly House and collected my axe. Then I went to the harbor and dialed Bub's number. He didn't answer. Next, I tried Jack at the manor, immediately hanging up on him after he told me that Bub wasn't there either. Then I steeled myself for the worst and coined off to the flat in Pandemonium.

I didn't have a key to Bub's homes, but I had never really needed one before. Jack was usually wherever we decided to stay. I didn't let that little drawback slow me down. I was all set to pull a Jenni and kick in the front door, but when the elevator opened, I found the door to the flat ajar.

I stepped inside without thinking. "Beelzebub?"

It could have been a trap. He could have been there with his new rebel companions. I was being reckless and not using my head, but I didn't care. I needed answers, and I needed them now.

The sitting room where Bub hosted his elaborate parties was tinted red from the hellish sky displayed through the wall of windows. The glass doors to the balcony stood open. Black curtains swayed in the sulfur-tinged wind, and tortured cries reached in from the Cocytus, the river of wailing souls that ran past Bub's building.

"Beelzebub!" I shouted again, running upstairs to the master bedroom.

"He's not here." Amy stepped out of the private bath.

I hadn't seen much of her since she and Gabriel had broken up. Her red hair was a tangled mess, and her spaded tail coiled nervously around her thigh, digging into her leather pants.

I blinked back a tear and swallowed. "Do you know where I can find him?"

She shook her head slowly. "I've been looking everywhere. He's missed a lot of committee meetings lately. At first, Cindy thought maybe he was skipping out on his duties to spend more time with you. But seeing you here, that's clearly not the issue." She bit her bottom lip. "I have a terrible premonition—"

"*No.*" I held my hand up and turned away from her. Seeing it was one thing, but hearing someone say it out loud… I wasn't ready for that.

I looked around the room, taking shallow breaths as I waited for my pulse to quiet. Everything was foreign—the black satin sheets I'd slept in, the blood-red walls I'd been pressed up against, the windows that wrapped halfway around the room. I hadn't stayed here with Bub in a while. I could tell that he hadn't frequented the place lately either. Withered petals were scattered around the base of a stone pot that had once held a rare black orchid.

Bub's priceless marble statue of Eve gave me a pitying look from the corner where the windowed walls met. She held her bitten apple out to me as if to show that she too had been baited and caught up in villainous wiles. I was in no mood for camaraderie.

"I'm not like you." I choked out a sob and raked my hands down my face. Eve's sin-stained lips seemed to deepen into a sneer.

"Lana?" Amy took a careful step toward me.

"I'm not like you!"

I crossed the room and swung my axe in a raging arc, amputating Eve's outstretched arm—apple and all. But I didn't stop there. I didn't stop until she was a million shattered pieces on the floor. I didn't stop until she was as broken as I felt.

CHAPTER SIXTEEN

"Experience: that most brutal of teachers.
But you learn, my God do you learn."
—C.S. Lewis

Destroying fine art is not a constructive way to overcome a broken heart, but it was the best I had time for. I knew the longer I waited to go to Grim, the more painful the meeting would be.

I considered my options on the way back to Reapers Inc. I could disappear into the mortal realm. I could run off to Summerland. I could tie a cement block to my ankles and jump into the sea. Everything seemed more pleasant than the looming threat of termination, or the looming threat of whatever it was I'd done to Craig, and Grim had done to Miranda. I wondered if Grim would take the time to torture me first.

I had lied by omission. I'd hindered the agenda against the rebels. That would be enough to make Grim question my loyalties and motives. I began to wonder how painful termination would be, and whether or not being *unexisted* would hurt more.

Ellen gave me a startled look as I stepped off the elevator and into the lobby of Reapers Inc.

"Is Grim in?" I glanced at his closed office door.

She nodded back slowly, her brows pulling up in solemn sympathy.

Grim's office was thick with smoke. When I walked in, he mashed a cigar out in a crowded ashtray on the corner of his desk. My eyes watered as I sat in one of the guest chairs. The grimace on his face was punctuated by surprise as he looked up.

"Harvey?" His coarse voice greeted me with suspicion, and his shoulders squared.

"Beelzebub has joined the rebels," I said hollowly, unable to meet his gaze.

Grim's jaw tightened. "So I've heard."

My insides coiled in on themselves as I waited for the inquisition. I stared blankly at Grim's chest, holding my breath.

He tapped his thick fingers on his desk. "How long have you known?"

"I thought I saw him with the rebels this afternoon. Then I ran into Amy at his flat in Pandemonium, and she confirmed my fear."

Grim clicked his tongue and assessed me with narrowed eyes. "And you had no clue before today?"

I looked down at my hands in my lap and shook my head, feeling my cheeks warm. All the signs seemed obvious now. Had I just not wanted to see them before?

Grim was quiet for the longest time. I closed my eyes and waited to see if I could feel a change. Did he have to touch me first? What would having my essence pulled out feel like? Could it be any worse than the way I already felt? Maybe if I hadn't been so fucked up, I would have had the sense to fight back. What would happen if the two of us tried to *unexist* each other at the same time? Maybe that was how reaper babies were made. Maybe I was losing my mind.

Grim finally killed my psychotic mental dialogue. "You're off special missions. The council simply won't have it. You can't be trusted."

It took all of my nerve to make eye contact with him. "I'm not with the rebels."

Grim pressed his lips together. "That really doesn't matter at this point. You know that, right? Every publication will be questioning it now. Which brings me to my next point." He cleared his throat. "You're not to speak a word of this to the press. I'll be making the official statement. Take tomorrow and Friday off. Once *Limbo's Laundry* comes out on Saturday, we'll hopefully be in the clear."

I blinked at him, my cheeks flaming more from confusion now.

Grim rolled his eyes. "Suspected rebels are not faring well in the city right now. The Demon Suffrage Movement has been buffering the assault on innocent demons, but I don't think you'll fall under their protection. In fact, they might see the lack of disciplinary action taken against you as an injustice."

I felt sick to my stomach. Not only had Bub broken my heart, damaged my reputation, and crippled my career but he'd also put me in the middle of a shitstorm without so much as an umbrella. Rage slowly ate away at my pain.

Grim went back to shuffling through files on his desk. "You've got two days to pull yourself together, Harvey. Make them count."

I should have been elated that I was still alive. I should have felt some sort of relief wash over me. I should have thanked Grim, not only for sparing me but also for wasting any time at all on damage control. Instead, misery and rage sank its hooks in even deeper.

When I opened Grim's door to leave, Jenni waited just outside, her expression stony and lethal. She'd heard every word.

"Jenni—"

"*Don't.*" She sidestepped around me and shut Grim's office door in my face.

The lobby was dark, and Ellen had gone home for the day. I swallowed my remorse and left, making my way to the harbor. I didn't feel like facing anyone. I didn't have answers for them. I didn't have answers for myself.

Two days. Make them count. What business was it of anyone's if I spent those days holed up on the ship, licking my wounds? Jenni would update Josie tonight, and she would take care of the unit during my absence.

The harbor was quiet when I arrived, and most of the reaper ferries had been docked for the evening, having already made their deliveries to the afterlives. The nephilim guards at the harbor travel booth watched me with weary eyes as I ventured farther down the dock. They'd be trading shifts with the night crew soon.

When I reached the ship, I hunted down a bottle of rum in the galley and then closed myself into the new cabin. The sheets were still unmade from my sleepover with Bub. I couldn't decide whether to gather them up and toss them into the sea or curl up in them and breathe in his lingering musk—campfire marshmallows and sulfur. I sat down at the desk and nursed the bottle of rum until the latter won out and I collapsed on the bed, sobbing myself into a restless sleep.

An hour later, a knock at the door stirred me. The most likely candidates were Josie and Gabriel. Maybe even Kevin. But my heart staggered at the irrational notion that it might be Bub. He wouldn't come to the harbor. Not now that he was a fugitive. Still, I pulled myself from the bed and answered the door. Just in case.

Maalik filled the doorway. His gray wings folded casually behind him, hands tucked into the pockets of his jean jacket. Dark curls hung in a ponytail over one shoulder, and a pitying smile played on his face as he took me in. "Hey."

"What are you doing here?" I wiped the back of my hand across my face, smearing tears and snot down my sleeve.

"I just came from a council meeting—"

"And you wanted to gloat, so you tracked me down. Is that it?"

"Hardly." He pulled his hands out of his pockets and stepped inside the cabin, closing the door behind him. "No one saw this coming. Not even me." He sighed. "I'm probably the one person on the council who absolutely believes in your innocence."

"You do?"

"Of course I do. Khadija would not have put her faith in someone unworthy."

"Stupid maybe, but at least I'm not unworthy." I laughed.

"Trusting. Not stupid." Maalik grinned. "I just wanted to make sure you were okay, and Gabriel said you weren't at Holly House."

"I'm not ready to deal with everyone yet. Why do you think I'm hiding out here?"

Maalik nodded. "Don't be discouraged. You've been a boon to the council, to Grim, this city—all of Eternity. They cannot fault you for failing to see the future. Especially when they cannot see it themselves."

It should have been weird and uncomfortable, having my ex check in on me. If he had been anyone else, I would have pegged him as a vulture, trying to catch me in a moment of weakness. But Maalik was better than that. I didn't have to hold my breath, anticipating his next move.

I shrugged. "I'm sure they're not the only ones who suspect me of being a double agent. Bub really dug himself a hole, and he almost buried me in it with him."

"Well, if it makes you feel any better, Cindy Morningstar has launched a sabotage campaign against him. His personal property is being seized and destroyed as we speak."

I wanted to be glad at the news, but it just made me feel worse. Like everything was somehow more final. More real. I didn't care about the flat in Pandemonium. I'd done my own sabotage work there. But my heart ached at the thought of the summer home in Tartarus. The Hell Committee would tear the place apart, along with my spare clothes in Bub's wardrobe, my toothbrush next to his by the bathroom sink, the hounds' chew toys on the floor. Everything came into sharp focus, and then the worst of it set in.

"Oh, gods." I pressed a hand to my chest.

Maalik touched my shoulder. "Lana? Are you all right?"

"I have to go to Tartarus. I have to warn Jack."

"You won't make it in time." Maalik's forehead crinkled. "And it's not safe for you to be there. The council will frown upon it, and your absolution could be compromised."

I pushed his hand away. "I don't care. I have to check on Jack."

"Then I'm going with you." Maalik opened the cabin door and waited for me to lead the way.

I was a little surprised at how quickly he'd given in, but then again, he knew me well enough by now to know he couldn't stop me. We rushed down the ramp of the ship and coined off to Tartarus.

CHAPTER SEVENTEEN

*"Love is a fire. But whether it is going to warm your
hearth or burn down your house, you can never tell."*
—*Joan Crawford*

Chunks of fiberglass were scattered along the beach as if
someone had taken a stick of dynamite to Bub's speedboat. I
squinted through the smoke toward the dock, and a sob
slipped from me. The houseboat was smoldering out its last
breath. Bits of charred boards crumbled into the river. My
knees quaked, but I stayed upright.

The damage to the manor was less permanent, but I still
flinched at the vulgarity of it. Big, neon orange letters scrawled
across the front door and over the stone and log exterior.
TRAITOR. EXILED. CREEDLESS FILTH. Every window
was haphazardly broken as if rocks had been thrown to get
the job done. Pale smoke drifted from a few, carrying a wet
staleness with it.

I ran past Maalik and up the steps to the front door, pushing it open without knocking. The foyer was a disaster.
Someone or something had dragged its claws down the walls,
crumbling up the plaster and slicing through paintings and
tapestries. The lights flickered like the wiring might have been
damaged in the process, and a dark substance was smeared

across the hardwood floor. I held my breath and tried not to gag.

The sound of clattering pots and pans drew me into the kitchen, where I found Jack hunkered over the sink, trying to lift a stock pot full of water. Smoke crept through the doorway leading to the dining room, and flames licked around the corner.

"Help me!" Jack strained under the weight of the pot. His fancy butler suit was torn and dirty. One horn was cracked from the tip all the way to his forehead. Dark blood leaked around the base of it and down his face. "Help me," he begged again.

I circled the counter, pulled the pot out of his hands, and ran into the dining room, tossing the water onto the worst of the flames. Maalik was right behind me with another pot. It only took two trips to put out the fire. But there would be more fires to come.

When we finished, I stopped Jack and made him sit down at the unscathed table in the kitchen. "You can't stay here. Bub's joined the rebels."

"Nonsense." Jack grimaced as he dabbed at his face with a handkerchief. I found his free hand and squeezed it, making him look at me.

"I saw it with my own eyes. I'm sorry, Jack."

All the betrayal I'd felt suddenly paled as I watched the old demon's face crumple. "No. It's another doppelganger, like that Loki fellow who tricked you over the summer."

I shook my head. "I was with Bub Monday. I *know* it was him. And Amy says he's been missing committee meetings longer than that."

Jack's expression was suddenly guarded. "You didn't see him yesterday?"

"No."

"He's never lied to me before," Jack said softly, twisting the handkerchief in his lap.

"Is there somewhere else you can stay?" Maalik asked, bringing us back to the immediacy of the situation.

Jack winced and gripped the edge of the table. "This is all I've ever known. I live to serve Master Beelzebub." He slumped forward with a moan.

"Jack?" I looked up at Maalik. "We need to get him out of here and to Meng's. That horn needs to be checked out, and he'll have a bed there until he can make other arrangements."

"What if they come back?" Jack slurred. "I have to be here to man the fort."

Maalik helped me stand him up. "This fort has been surrendered. You're being honorably discharged."

Jack's snort was cut through with a sharp inhale. "What am I going to do?" His eyelids drooped closed as his head lolled onto my shoulder, his broken horn oozing blood onto my sleeve.

Maalik and I looped our arms under his and drag-stepped him back through the foyer, carefully avoiding the dark spots on the floor. Angry voices filtered in to us from beyond the broken windows, and panic picked up my pace. Maalik heard them too and gave me a worried frown.

"I can fly. Let me take the demon—"

"*Jack*," I snapped.

Maalik clenched his teeth. "Let me take *Jack*, and you make a run for the coin border."

I didn't like it, but I didn't have a better plan. There was no telling how many demons waited outside. I helped Maalik reposition Jack so he could hook his arms under Jack's armpits. Then I dug a coin out of my pocket and crept up to the door to squint through the peephole. "It's clear for now."

Maalik grunted under Jack's weight as he stepped up beside me. "Don't bother looking for them. Just run. I'll meet you at the harbor."

I wrapped my hand around the doorknob and shuddered as adrenaline surged through me. Maalik nodded, and I jerked the door open.

I took the walkway steps three at a time. Maalik's shadow zipped ahead, but then circled back, urging me to keep up. Shouts rang out, announcing our location. I ducked my head down and leapt from the edge of the path, sliding into the scorching sand as if I were aiming for a home run. Dust clouded around me. I didn't wait for it to settle. I rolled my coin and tumbled face-first onto the harbor dock.

"Lana?" Maalik landed more gracefully beside me, an unconscious Jack slumped in his arms.

"I'm fine." I sat up and dusted the sand from my jeans.

"We need to move. They could come looking for us here."

"We can take the travel booths to Meng's." I stood and grabbed Jack's feet.

Maalik's brows dipped into an irritated line. "I came here tonight to offer sympathy and encouragement. I certainly didn't expect this."

"I'm just tons of fun." I gave him a tight smile, angling sideways so we could both see where we were walking as we hauled Jack down the pier.

Darkness had settled in, and the air was damp, making the dusting of sand on my skin extra gritty. It tickled along my arms and worked its way through my clothes to mingle with the sweat I was working up.

The lanterns along the dock swayed in the breeze, their halos of light dancing across the old boards. Boats creaked and sloshed in their slips. The sea sounded anxious tonight. Heavy waves rocked up against the seawall as if something ominous was creeping in with the tide.

The nephilim guards at the entrance to the dock tilted their spears toward us as we neared. They probably thought we were trying to dispose of a dead body. One guard moved in front of the travel booth just beyond the dock, blocking the entrance.

Maalik stepped under a lantern, letting the light spill over his face. "Our friend needs medical attention."

"Councilman," the second guard bowed his head in greeting and nudged his partner, who stood steadfast before the booth.

"We'll need to see his visa," he said sharply.

Maalik's eyes swirled with hellfire. "As a council member, I am allowed to vouch for visitors. Perhaps you need to reread the Nephilim Guard handbook."

The guard scowled as he stepped out of the way, fluttering his small wings abruptly. His intimidation efforts fell flat, considering how many times I'd seen Gabriel and Maalik do the same on a much larger scale. I resisted the urge to *attaboy* him and fumbled with Jack's feet as Maalik turned to back into the booth. Once we were crammed inside, I set Jack's feet down so I could find my coin again.

The booths had seemed a bit old-fashioned at first, but they were quickly upgrading. The manual clicker cameras had been replaced by newer video surveillance, and the travel system now accepted Bank of Eternity debit cards. I dropped my coin into the slot and selected the stop near Meng's on the touchscreen monitor. The glass darkened as the booth whirred and then cleared a second later.

Divine Boulevard was empty. A symphony of crickets and owls called out from the woods circling Meng's temple off the southern coast. The path through the trees was poorly lit, and Maalik and I both stumbled along the way. My missteps were more pronounced than his, without wings to catch my fall. We found our way more easily once we reached the clearing.

Light blazed through the temple's screened walls and reflected off the pond in the front garden, where bullfrogs greeted us with nervous croaks. We climbed the front steps, and I dropped one of Jack's ankles to ring Meng's bell. A murmur of voices spilled out to us when Jai Ling, Meng's child soul assistant, answered the door.

A dirty apron was fastened over her dress, and the smile she welcomed us with was soon erased when she saw Jack. "Another one?"

I ignored her annoyed tone. "Please tell me you have an open bed."

Jai Ling's nose crinkled as she opened the door all the way and waved us inside. Jack stirred in our arms as we crossed the threshold.

"I'm going to be late picking up Master's dry-cleaning," he mumbled.

My stomach knotted as a portly demon emerged from the hallway. He glared at us as he walked past, angling his bandaged arm away defensively. Grim's words slapped me in the face, and I wondered just how many battered and bitter demons Meng was housing tonight.

Jai Ling directed us into a small, partitioned room. Thin curtains cut the space in half, taking it from cozy to stoic. The side we were led to had a small bed pushed up against one wall. We had just tucked Jack in when Meng arrived.

She wore a stained apron like Jai Ling's, but her pockets were blooming with an assortment of medieval tools that looked like they would have been right at home in a torture chamber. Apparently, not everything could be fixed with her nasty tea.

"My favorite reaper," she cackled, then followed it up with a groan as her eyes fell on Jack. "Lucky I like you." She waved a crooked finger at me as she leaned over to inspect his busted horn.

"Can you fix it?" I massaged the strained muscles in my shoulder and noticed the crusted demon blood on my sleeve. I had a tank top on underneath, so I peeled off my shirt and tossed it into the wastebasket by the door.

Meng's lips pinched together. "This fly master's servant?"

"Yes." I cringed at the implication. "He had no idea. That's why he was still at…the manor when it was attacked."

I just couldn't get Bub's name past the lump that formed in my throat every time I thought of him.

Meng patted my arm with a gentle smile. "I take good care of him."

A moan from the room across the hall caught her attention, and she shooed Jai Ling off to help before setting to work cleaning Jack's horn. I left her to her magic and followed Maalik out into the hall.

Every room we passed looked as if it had been divided to fit more patients. Several demons sat in mismatched chairs around the foyer, waiting their turn. Most of their injuries seemed less pressing. A busted lip. A broken talon. Still, most of them glared accusingly at us, resentful that we'd bypassed the line.

Maalik walked with me to Holly House. He didn't spout off any chivalrous garbage about it being for my own good, so I didn't comment on his wide, darting eyes. I was a little on edge myself.

"Well," he said, killing the awkward silence. "I didn't know Meng had a favorite anything. She's certainly warmed right up to you."

"Only because I helped persuade the Fates to incorporate her tea in their factory lineup."

"That's right. I almost forgot. Your ambition is a force of its own these days."

I bit my tongue and picked up the pace, willing the walk and conversation to be over soon. The disorder between us had finally settled into something manageable, and I didn't want to spoil it yet.

Maalik's hand wrapped around my shoulder. "I'm sorry. I didn't mean for that to sound so crass."

I stopped in front of Holly House and turned to give him a forced smile. "I know."

We stood under the streetlight for a moment, both fidgeting nervously as we stared at each other. The absence of the romantic tension that had once marked our partings was uncomfortably profound.

Maalik was first to break the silence again. "That was a kind thing of you to do for that demon—*Jack*," he quickly amended.

"He's done nothing wrong, and he's a good person."

Maalik nodded and gave me a weak smile. "Take care, Lana."

"You, too." I let out a long breath I hadn't realized I'd been holding.

Maalik waited, watching me cross the courtyard to the front door. I didn't have the energy to be annoyed. I punched in my door code and gave him a farewell nod as I ducked in-side.

Charlie glanced up from the front desk with an uneasy smile. I was sure I looked like hell. I felt even worse.

Staying on the ship didn't seem like a good idea anymore. Though having another run-in with Jenni wasn't something I was interested in either. I stepped inside an elevator and stared at the buttons, my finger hovering over the ten. At the last second, I changed my mind and punched the five.

CHAPTER EIGHTEEN

"If everything isn't black and white,
I say, why the hell not?"
—John Wayne

It was creeping up on midnight, but at least I didn't have to worry about waking Gabriel's roommate, the captain of the Nephilim Guard. He worked nights. Gabriel said it was Ross's choice. That if the rebels attacked the city, he wanted to be there, and they were most likely to strike under the cover of night.

I rang Gabriel's doorbell twice before he answered in a pair of frayed drawstring pants.

"Lana?" He blinked stiffly against the bright hall lights and rubbed the sleep from his eyes. "You wanna come in?"

I nodded and slipped past him. Gabriel gently closed the door, mindful of his slumbering neighbors. When he turned around, I lost it. The seal on my tsunami of hurt and rage burst. I stood in his dining room and sobbed like the world was ending.

Gabriel wrapped his arms around me, sweeping his wings up my back to form a feathery cocoon. He tucked my head under his chin and held me tightly, letting my tears run down his chest.

"Do you want to talk about it?"

"No." I hiccupped. "Maybe—*no.* No, I don't."

"Okay." He stroked my hair.

"Go ahead. Say it. I know you want to."

"Say what?"

"That you told me so. That this is what I get for not listening. That I should have expected this if I was going to date a demon."

Gabriel sighed. "Do you want a beer?"

I nodded against his chest. "Do you think Ross will mind if I crash on your couch tonight?"

"You can have my bed. I'll leave him a note, so you don't get a spear in the face." He peeled himself away from me and went to the refrigerator to fetch us a couple of Ambrosia Ales. "I thought you might stay on the ship tonight. Josie said you did Monday—" He winced, probably remembering the rest of Josie's words, how Bub had stayed with me.

Tears clouded my eyes again, but I blinked them back and nodded. "Kevin finished remodeling the new cabin."

"Hey, how 'bout some good news?" He set one of the ales on the counter so he could twist the cap off the other and hand it to me. "You're off the Hypnos search party. That's got to be a relief, right?"

I shrugged. "Except for the part where Jenni hates me."

"She'll get over it. She's got Josie to help her now. Who's totally in your corner, by the way." He opened his own ale and tapped it against mine before taking a long drink from his bottle. I did the same, letting his words sink in.

"*Wait.* So you've known about this Hypnos nonsense all along?"

Gabriel raised an eyebrow. "On the Board of Heavenly Hosts, remember?"

"And now Josie knows everything that I was forbidden to tell her?" My anger was muted by relief. I could talk to her about it now. The question was, could she speak with me?

Gabriel nodded slowly. "I suppose. Grim informed the council of the special missions change earlier this evening. Then Holly called to update me." He looked bothered at the mention of our most holy landlord. "She seemed rather proud to know so much about my nearest and dearest."

"Sorry. Rules." Secrets were getting really annoying.

"Josie said you've become a stickler about those lately."

"I can remember a time when you would have said that about *her.*" I snorted and took another drink.

"Speaking of rules, Holly's ego is rather handy. I'm sure she shares more than Grim would approve of. I'm just glad the board is so exclusive, and that so much seems to go over her head. I'm pretty sure she still thinks the special missions' objective is to smoke out some hidden rebel base."

"If not from Holly, then how do you know Hypnos was Grim's focus?"

He grinned. "A little history lesson Saul taught me long before you came along."

"Enlighten me."

Gabriel grabbed two more beers from the refrigerator and waved me into the living room. The television was frozen on a shot of John Wayne and Marguerite Churchill from the

Big Trail. A monstrous black sofa filled most of the room, and a coffee table cluttered with snacks and magazines completed the otherwise unadorned bachelor pad.

I kicked off my boots and curled up on the couch, propping my feet on Gabriel's lap. He rested his hand on my shin then pulled it away, rubbing sand between his fingers with a puzzled look.

"Don't change the subject." I nudged his thigh with my toes.

"Right." Gabriel shook his head. "Hypnos…"—he paused dramatically, lifting his chin in the air—"is Grim's brother."

"What?"

"That's right. *Grim* Thanatos." He gave me a sharp look. "You probably shouldn't call him that, though. He quit using his real name when he founded the council to promote anonymity."

I rolled my eyes. "Well, it didn't take. Someone remembers, and I'm guessing that's why Hypnos was taken."

"Yeah, but there's not much Grim can do about it without looking like he's using valuable resources for his own personal agenda since Hypnos isn't exactly crucial to the Fates' factory. Especially after Meng's recent contribution."

"So that's why he's convinced the council that Jenni is out there looking for a secret base instead?"

Gabriel laughed. "*Convinced* probably isn't the right word."

I didn't feel any better about the situation, but at least it made sense now. I hadn't really ever given Grim's history much thought. I couldn't imagine him in flowing Greek robes—or in anything but the sharp angles of a business suit.

As my mind wrapped around the new vision of my boss, more blanks started to fill in. "Hypnos's cave is in Tartarus."

Gabriel took another drink and nodded.

"Beelzebub was the new recruit the rebels were talking about," I said, more to myself than Gabriel. "He's the one who took Hypnos."

"Well, I'll be." Gabriel's eyes went wide as he stared off into space.

Even though we had patched things up, it was difficult talking to Gabriel about Bub. Since his split with Amy, it was easier to just skip over the relationship small talk altogether. Still, when Bub weighed heavily on my mind, I found myself desperately longing for Gabriel's perspective, as biased as it might be.

I shifted on the couch. "So, which council members are calling for my head on a platter?"

"Ridwan," he grumbled.

"Of course."

"Of course." Gabriel tilted his head to one side, eyebrows drawing together as he thought. "Horus is in your favor, though his sincerity is questionable. Same thing with Meng. Your alliances are definitely paying off. Maalik's vow of your innocence might be sincere, but as your former companion, his opinion holds even less weight. According to Holly, everyone else is staying neutral. For now."

I finished my beer and traded the empty bottle for the fresh one Gabriel handed me. The television flickered off, having remained paused for too long. We sat quietly in the dark, sipping beer and taking turns sighing over the frustration and despair of it all.

"I saw Amy today," I said.

"Oh?" Gabriel's face creased. He looked down at the bottle in his hand and sloshed the last swallow around the bottom rim before nudging my feet away to stand.

"I ran into her in Pandemonium—at Bub's flat. Cindy sent her to track him down."

Gabriel's shoulders hunched as he walked to the refrigerator and pulled out two more ales. "I haven't seen her since…"

"Sorry."

"Don't be. It's for the best," he said softly.

Gabriel and Amy's breakup had gone mostly unnoticed by the media. I was sure it made working with Peter and Holly easier, but they were probably the only two who seriously thought it was *for the best*.

I kept my opinion to myself and snuggled into Gabriel as he joined me on the couch again. He dug the remote out from under a half-eaten bag of Cheetos and turned John Wayne back on the big screen, propping his feet up on the coffee table.

"I miss this." I laid my head on his lap and curled my knees up to my stomach.

Gabriel spun one of my curls around his finger. "Me, too."

CHAPTER NINETEEN

"I find hope in the darkest of days, and focus in the brightest.
I do not judge the universe."
—*Dalai Lama*

I woke up in Gabriel's bed Thursday morning with the hang-over of the century. Between the rum on the ship and then the Ambrosia Ale, I smelled like the sticky bathroom floor of Purgatory Lounge.

Gabriel was gone, but he'd left a note tucked under a package of powdered donuts and a cup of coffee. The luke-warm brew helped me gauge his departure time at about half an hour earlier.

I took my time moving around, careful not to make too much noise. I could hear Ross snoring down the hall in his room. It was a deep, throaty sound that I imagined worked well as an alarm for Gabriel. I didn't see one in his room, just a square wall clock hanging above a desk covered in a layer of wadded-up paper. He'd be getting a new trashcan for Christ-mas this year.

I waited until nine, and then I left Gabriel's and took the elevator up to the tenth floor. It was nice having the condo to myself for a change. I brushed my teeth and took a hot shower, scrubbing away the last of the sand. It felt engrained in my skin, clinging to me as fiercely as the memory of Bub's ruined home.

When I was done, I wrapped myself in a robe and fixed a cup of tea at the breakfast bar, zoning in and out of conscious thought. *Two days. Make them count.*

Would two days really fix this? Was I supposed to have all the answers, all the closure that I needed? Or just enough to function?

Most of the day slipped by without much effort on my part. There was a hollow throbbing in my chest. I just wanted to sleep for the next ten years, or at least until the rebels were finally wiped out. Then I could wake up and pretend like none of it had ever happened. Like I was an ordinary reaper. Like I'd never even met the Lord of the Flies.

Around five, a set of keys jingled at the front door. I jumped up, ready to run for the cover of my room, but I wasn't fast enough.

Josie's head popped around the door as it opened. "Hey! I was hoping I'd catch you." She glanced down at my fuzzy slippers.

"What are you doing home so early?" I ran a hand through my curls and eased back onto the barstool.

She held up a handful of files. "Paperwork. Grim has me filling in while you're out, and I don't have an office. The kitchen table will have to do."

"You could have used my office."

Josie shrugged. "I also wanted to see if you were home. I know you're off duty right now, but would you mind looking over everything after I fill it out?"

"Yeah, sure."

"Also, um…" She sat down on the barstool next to me and dropped the stack of files on the counter, watching to see if I would steal a peek. When I didn't right away, she darted her eyes down and back up at me.

Jenni's handwriting was scrawled across the file on top. *Friday, 9am.* I looked away.

Josie touched my arm. "I'm working special missions with Jenni now. Do you want an update?" she asked gently.

"You shouldn't—"

"Why? Are you going to go tell the rebels?"

I stared at her wide-eyed.

"Didn't think so." She folded her hands over the counter. "First of all, that bat out of hell that chased you two around Salacia's resort was Sharur, the smasher of thousands."

I crinkled my nose.

"The Sumerian war god Ninurta's enchanted mace?" she added, shaking her head when recognition still didn't dawn on me.

"Lots of old gods have been coming out of the soul matter lately. That's nothing new."

Josie nodded. "Except Ninurta isn't with the rebels. Just his bespelled weapon of choice. It just up and left him one day, went out looking for trouble."

I huffed. "Well, it sure found it."

"We have it in custody now."

"Grim's seriously going to interrogate an animated object?"

Josie barked out a laugh. "Right. No, we're going to implant a tracking device on it and *accidentally* let it escape."

"Smart."

"Jenni and I will be following it tomorrow morning." She tapped the mission file. "Bub might be waiting wherever it leads."

"I know." I picked at the hem of my sleeve.

"How are you holding up?"

I looked away from her. The lump in my throat had returned, and my eyes stung.

Josie rubbed a hand over my back. "That demon cab driver finally spilled his guts."

I made a disgusted face, even though she had only meant it figuratively. It was probably a far more literal statement than she needed to know.

"He revealed the name of the factory worker who's been aiding the rebels. Grim has the soul in custody now too."

It sounded like the thirty-seventh floor was staying busy. Maybe that's why Grim had spared me. Torture and interrogation can be so tiresome.

Josie fingered the stack of files. "The Nephilim Guard is keeping a better eye on the abandoned resort and the coast in general. The rebels' water sirens have found a way to bypass the barrier reef and open a portal right in the water. Kinda like you did last summer."

"I had a sanctioned Latin hall pass."

Josie lowered her voice. "You could always ask your *special friend* how they're doing it. You know. The one who *knows* things."

I clasped my hands in my lap and looked down. Josie didn't ask about Winston often. Probably because she knew how difficult it had been for me to tell her about him in the first place.

"The travel booths have mucked things up in that department. I haven't seen him in a while." She didn't need to know about Naledi yet.

"Well, maybe one of those scaly bitches swiped a relic or something. Maybe the wards on the sea were tampered with. We'll figure it out eventually."

It would have been nice to just ask Winston for an explanation. Of course, he'd probably have to go buy Naledi a knickknack and fan her with a palm leaf for a while first. Barf. It was amazing how little tolerance I had for sweetness when my insides felt so rotten.

I didn't realize I was scowling until Josie started rubbing my back again. "You'll get through this. You're too stubborn to let it keep you down for long." She scooped up her paperwork and offered a small smile. "I better get started on this. Kevin will be home with the hounds in a bit. He's bringing pizza if you'd like to join us."

I hesitated. "Is Jenni eating with you, too?"

Josie dipped her head in a short nod.

"Does she still hate me?"

"She was pretty angry at first, but I think she understands why you didn't say anything. You had to be sure. I would have done the same if it were Kevin."

"Rain check on dinner?" I stood and hugged myself. "I think I just need a little alone time tonight."

Josie gave me a sad smile and nodded. "Sure. Maybe to-morrow?"

"Yeah. That'd be nice."

I sulked back to my room and closed the door before curling up on my bed in the fetal position. I really didn't know what to do with myself. Sitting around feeling pathetic wasn't doing much good, but without work and Bub, my life was pretty boring. Dinner with the gang had too much potential of turning into a pity party, and I'd had all the sorry looks I could stomach for now.

I dialed Meng's number. Jai Ling answered on the second ring. "Lady Meng's Teahouse—not to be confused with a hospital or safe house. How may I help you?"

"Jai, it's Lana. I just wanted to check in on Jack."

"Jack? Oh, you mean the old curmudgeon demon you brought in?"

"That's the one."

An indignant throat clearing sounded in the background. Jai Ling sighed. "He's right here."

"Lana, my dear. I am in your debt," Jack bubbled. "The horn is mending nicely, thanks to Lady Meng's healing touch."

"That's great."

"And she's even offered me room and board in exchange for taking over the cooking and cleaning duties. Apparently, her *current* help is inadequate."

I heard Jai Ling snort.

"Well, look at you. And here I was, trying to figure out what I should tell my roommates when they asked about the demon on our couch."

"You're too kind, but I couldn't possibly stay at Holly House. My reputation is soiled enough as it is," he said sadly.

"How are Meng's demon guests treating you?"

Jack paused. "Better, now that they know I was wrongfully mistaken for a rebel."

"Yeah, the city doesn't seem like a very safe place for your brethren lately."

"Indeed." Jack huffed. "But Meng has one of the Nephilim Guard on retainer if I should need to venture beyond the safety of the temple."

"That's good to know." I bit my lip and sucked in a slow breath. "Has he tried to contact you?"

Jack's voice darkened. "No."

I rubbed a hand over my collarbone, trying to push away the dread boiling to the surface. I just couldn't understand why, but I wanted to so badly.

Jack sighed into the phone. "It's best if we both put him out of our minds. He clearly knew that neither of us would follow him to the rebels."

"Too bad we didn't know him that well."

After I said goodnight to Jack, I heard the hounds bellow out a greeting from the dining room. I cracked my door, so they would be able to get in after they'd eaten dinner. Then I went to bed early. If I had two days off work, the least I could accomplish was catching up on sleep.

CHAPTER TWENTY

"Our greatest glory is not in never falling,
but in rising every time we fall."
—Confucius

Thursday melted into Friday, in between scattered sleep that I woke from, crying more often than not. Coreen went to work with Kevin, but Saul stayed in bed with me. He whimpered and nuzzled himself under my arm, draping his slobbery jowls over my shoulder and tickling my ear with his dog breath.

From my bedroom window, I could see across the top of the entire city, all the way to where a flock of ghostly storks was departing from the factory. They circled the park, just above the trees that had begun to change colors, and then ascended into the clouds, off to deliver recycled souls to the mortal realm.

Around noon, Saul's whimpering became more from hunger than sympathy. He licked my hand and turned his big pitiful eyes up at me. I found the energy to pull myself out of bed long enough to throw some food into his bowl and eat a slice of cold pizza. Then we snuggled up on the couch with some John Wayne.

Josie came home early again, sporting a nasty shiner and an even nastier attitude. "Please tell me you're coming back to work tomorrow." Her face puckered into a full-on pout as she slapped her paperwork down on the kitchen table.

"That's the plan." I grabbed a couple of beers from the refrigerator and waited for her to answer my questioning stare.

"You ever been punched by a soul?" she asked, taking a can from me and gently rolling it across her puffy eye.

I leaned in to take a closer look. "Can't say that I have."

She pulled the can away and tilted her head to give me a better view. "Yeah, and this jerk was actually on the list for Heaven. Guess he was expecting Jesus to make a special trip just for him. Luckily, I didn't accidentally kick him over the deck railing."

"I thought you were working with Jenni today."

"Just this morning." Her scowl deepened. "Just long enough to watch a possessed mace disappear under the sea and blip right off our radar, like it had found the fucking Bermuda Triangle."

I cringed. "That sucks."

"Yup." She cracked open her beer and chugged it. Foam dribbled down her chin, and she wiped it away with the back of her hand. "And what the hell is up with Grim's obsession with Hypnos? Like that old fart is doing the rebels any good."

"Gabriel says he's Grim's brother."

"What?" Josie slammed her beer down on the counter and ran a hand through her short hair. "So we don't even really know if Hypnos is being kept at a rebel base? They could have dumped him in the sea, and we're running around like we're searching for the Holy Grail? This is ridiculous."

I held my hands up. "I totally agree."

"And here I was jealous that Jenni had chosen you over me for this *vital* task," she scoffed.

I patted her on the back, half in jest and half in earnest.

My feelings about Jenni's special missions were a conflicted mess. I was glad that the decision wasn't on me, because I wouldn't have known where to begin. The council wanted me off special missions because they didn't trust me. I didn't trust myself either, but for very different reasons.

Working with Jenni was probably my best bet at running into Bub. My first impulse at his betrayal had been to track him down and demand answers, and the urge was still strongly present. But Bub didn't want to be found, and he'd probably just take off again if I did happen to come across him.

There was also the gut-wrenching fear that I'd have to watch Jenni kill him—since I certainly wasn't capable of it. Not yet anyway. I was hurt and angry, but I didn't want him to die. I wanted Jack to be right about a doppelganger being in his place. I wanted Bub to show up at my door and tell me it had all been a horrendous lie. I wanted him to hold me and convince me that I was ridiculous for thinking him capable of such things.

When I wasn't fantasizing about Bub white-knighting my problems away, I agonized over just how evil he had become. It seemed so tragically comic. Just how evil was the prince of demons these days? I knew I wasn't capable of killing him, but I also didn't think I could stand by and watch him hurt Jenni. And now I had Josie to worry about, too.

My own safety was too abstract to think on for long. I just couldn't imagine Bub trying to physically harm me, which was ridiculous, seeing as how he had no problem carrying out the emotional slaughter.

My time off felt wasted on a concoction of useless feelings and unanswered questions, and it was over entirely too soon. I felt like I'd been given a cough drop for the plague.

My evaluation with Grim Saturday morning was nothing special. I had built up an unhealthy amount of dread—even more so than when I'd confessed to seeing Bub with the rebels. Grim asked half a dozen mundane questions, and then he stamped my file and told me to turn it in to Ellen.

I began the day with my head down, hoping to muscle through the workload and find relief in the form of distraction. Any downtime felt like a reminder of how broken I was inside. I passed out the dockets and took the hounds with me, sending Kevin and the new recruits with Josie. I knew I was making a lousy impression as unit captain to Molly and Tyler, but I just didn't care.

Harvesting mass souls with the Posy Unit didn't allow for as much soul interaction as the freelance harvesting I used to do. It all felt so impersonal. The souls talked among themselves instead of to me. I admit the hooded robe wasn't very inviting, but when we were one-on-one, they usually worked up the nerve to make conversation. Today, I would have settled for a fist fight. Josie had all the fun.

I didn't loiter at the office after work. Ellen was acting oddly uncomfortable around me, and it hurt to think she might suspect me of being a traitor. I finished my paperwork and hurried home, ready to swallow the final pill of the week and get it over with. *Limbo's Laundry* was out today.

Josie had the magazine spread out on the kitchen counter when I walked in. Jenni and Kevin sat on either side of her, reading over her shoulder.

"Dirty, rotten bastards," she grumbled, slapping a center-fold image of the smoking ruins of Bub's summer home. "They're trying to pin this catastrophe on you. They're even claiming that you destroyed some priceless sculpture at the flat in Pandemonium."

My stomach knotted. "I did, actually."

Josie's head jerked up. Jenni and Kevin turned accusing faces toward me too, and I blushed.

"I'm not responsible for the country home, though," I said quickly.

Josie pulled her wide eyes away from me and shook her head. "Well, the article's not very flattering, but I think it's working in your favor anyway. No one suspects that you're with the rebels anymore."

"Yay for small victories?" I tugged the magazine out from under her hand and skimmed the article. She was right. It wasn't very flattering.

There was a picture of me fleeing Bub's smoking manor. Maalik and I had thought we were escaping vandals, but it had just been reporters looking to get a statement from Bub before he was officially excommunicated from the council's good graces. Instead, they got a picture of me running from the scene of a crime.

I looked back up at my roommates and watched them shift nervously under my gaze.

"I went back for Jack," I said, pointing out the compromising picture.

Josie and Jenni exchanged skeptical looks.

"Seriously, guys? Maalik was with me. We thought those reporters were demons coming to wreak more havoc. We were running for our lives."

They didn't look convinced.

"Hey, no need to explain yourself to us." Josie held her hands up and leaned back. "I'd totally destroy Kevin's shit if he betrayed me."

Kevin looked up at her. "Destroy my stuff? What are you talking about? You'd kill me dead if I betrayed you."

Josie shrugged. "Yeah, but I'd break your bow in half first—before beating you to death with it."

I groaned. "Guys, I did not do this." I jabbed my finger at the magazine again. "The statue happened right after I found out, but I *loved* that house." My voice broke as I welled up.

"Okay." Josie nudged my arm. "We were just teasing."

A knock on the door ended the conversation, and Gabriel let himself in. He had a bag of Cheetos tucked in the crook of one arm, a six-pack of Ambrosia Ale in one hand, and a deck of cards in the other.

"If you have plans tonight, cancel them," he said, dumping his loot on the kitchen table. "I hereby call this surprise poker game to order."

Kevin stood and walked around the counter to dig a bowl out of the dishwasher. "Is it just the five of us?"

"Four." Jenni pulled her jacket off the back of her stool and went to the front door. "I've got some work to catch up on at the office. Have fun."

Jenni and I weren't quite right yet, but we were getting there. She wasn't giving me the silent treatment anymore, so there was that. I think, more than anything, she was angry that I was off special missions. I had no way of knowing that Bub would jump the fence, but it still felt like Jenni blamed me for dating him in the first place. Like none of this would have happened if I'd just played by the unspoken rules.

Maybe she was right.

CHAPTER TWENTY-ONE

*"A lie will go round the world
while truth is pulling its boots on."*
—Charles Spurgeon

The weekend slipped by uneventfully. I felt like a zombie, going through the motions on autopilot. My new and improved aura created a fearsome reaction in my harvests. Not a single soul crossed me. I felt like the true epitome of Death. The image had a certain air of respect about it, but it wasn't me, and I hoped it wouldn't last.

Before I knew it, it was Monday. The small bit of recovery I'd made was overshadowed by the creeping anxiety I felt when I remembered Beelzebub's demon defense class I was supposed to substitute for.

The academy didn't open until five, after most reapers were done harvesting for the day. The night classes fit better into everyone's schedule, though there were still a few high-risk reapers who harvested around the clock.

When I called the main office, the academy secretary quickly transferred me to Grace Adaline.

"Has the demon defense class been canceled?" I asked.

"Not as of yet. Are you a student?" Grace didn't recognize my voice. I was surprised, considering what a pain I had been in her class the previous semester.

"No, I'm supposed to substitute tonight. I really thought it would be canceled, though. Are you sure?"

"Ah, Ms. Harvey. Yes, your name is written down here."

"So, I should still come in then?" I was practically whining.

"If you wouldn't mind, dear. The school board hasn't had the chance to address the recent…complications, but we do believe this is a valuable course for reapers. We'll have the issue settled by next week."

"Okay."

I could get through one night. Couldn't I?

With everything that had happened, I really hadn't thought to prepare for the class. Bub had assigned essays, so I could collect those. Otherwise, I didn't have a clue. I was more concerned about the accusing stares I was sure to be on the receiving end of. A whole room full of them. Super.

I dragged my feet on the way to the academy, waiting until the very last minute to enter the classroom. Showing up early would have given someone the brilliant idea to ask me questions that were none of their business.

The room was abuzz, though only about half of the enrolled students were in attendance. I wasn't the only one who had assumed the class would be canceled. It was hard telling which reapers were truly interested in the course, and which ones had just shown up for the sake of gossip. My shoulders sagged when I realized that Kevin was absent. It hadn't even occurred to me to ask if he'd be dropping the class.

A stillness fell over the room as I sat down in the instructor's chair. Voices faded off into a hushed murmur. A student in the front row took the lead and brought his essay up, setting it neatly on the corner of the desk. A few students had trouble making eye contact with me as they turned in their essays, but they all found the nerve to look up from their desks in anticipation once they were seated again. The pressure was suffocating. I had to get out of there.

I decided to pull a Jack and instructed them to read from the *Ars Goetia* mentioned on the extended reading list. "There are seventy-two demons Solomon invoked to build his temple. Memorize them." I stood and scooped up the pile of essays.

"Why? The professor's gone AWOL. What's the point?" A skinny little twit along the back row folded her arms and openly glared at me. I recognized her at once as Miss Bubblegum Ponytail from the first day of class.

I glanced down at the roster and tried to recall her actual name. "Lacey Irmen?"

"I'm touched you remember." She put a hand to her chest in mock flattery.

I had no witty comeback. I just wasn't in the mood. "Your first test will be next week. It's over Solomon's demons. If your essay sucks and you fail the test, you'll be cut from the class. That's the point, Ms. Irmen."

She snorted and turned to rant to another student as she collected her books. "If I'd known some holier-than-thou eighth-generation reaper would be teaching this course, I wouldn't have bothered signing up. If the Lord of the Flies is with the rebels, who's to say he even trained her properly?"

I stuffed the essays into my bag and left before anyone else worked up the courage to mouth off.

As I rushed past the front office, Grace Adaline called out to me, running to catch my arm before I reached the front doors. "Can I have a word with you, Ms. Harvey?"

I cringed but nodded. Grace had been of the same generation as my mentor, Saul Avelo. And she had given me a passing grade in her wandering souls class, which made it possible for me to join the Posy Unit in the first place and stave off Horus's blackmail threats.

"I'd like to talk to you about the possibility of being an adjunct professor."

Voices spilled out into the hall as the demon defense students left the classroom. Grace, noticing my look of panic, put a hand on my back and steered me into her office. She closed the door and pointed at one of the chairs in front of her desk.

"We really need this class in our curriculum, and you're the only reaper who has been fully trained in demon defense."

"Why not hire another demon to teach it?"

Grace frowned. "Demons aren't exactly coming to the city in droves lately, and rapport between reapers and demons is at an all-time low. Hiring one would result in a significant drop in attendance."

It was hard to hide my disgust. "So we're just going to start shunning them now? Because they need another reason to join the rebels?"

Grace sighed and propped her chin in her hand. "I don't like it either, but the academy is a business, and businesses need revenue. We have to keep the student body's reservations in mind."

I folded my arms and slouched back in the chair. "I don't know that my rapport with other reapers is going to help attendance right now either."

Grace nodded as she considered my words. "Maybe." Then she held up a copy of *Limbo's Laundry*. "Maybe not. What reaper would doubt a demon defense professor who has the audacity to seek vengeance on her traitorous demon lover? Especially a demon of Beelzebub's magnitude."

I chewed my bottom lip and looked out Grace's office window at the students coming and going. "I'm in my first year as a mentor, and my first year on a specialty unit—as the *captain*. When I really take the time to wrap my mind around it all, I'm proud and amazed that I've lasted this long." I looked back at Grace. "I don't want to push my luck."

Grace looked disappointed, as if she had hoped I was coming to the opposite conclusion, that I was strong and capable enough to keep biting off more than I could chew.

"At least take some time to think about it," she said, standing to walk me out.

I gave her a weak smile and bit my tongue out of respect. If anyone else had asked, my answer would have been a simple, direct *"hell, no."*

Twilight was creeping upon the city as I left. A small herd of students gathered around the travel booth off Tombstone Drive, so I hooked a right on Council Street and headed south on Westwood Road, toward the booth on Morte Avenue.

When I made it back to the condo, Josie was in the kitchen. She sat at the breakfast bar, eating a bowl of corn-flakes in her flannel pajamas. Her hair was wet from a recent shower and spiked out in a glossy halo around her head. The bruise circling her eye had faded to a dirty yellow.

"Dinner of champions?" I grinned.

"Dinner of the tired and lazy," she said around a mouthful of cereal. She swallowed and glanced over my shoulder. "Where's Kevin?"

"I don't know." I closed the door and set my bag on the kitchen table. "He wasn't in class."

Josie's face twisted into a scowl. "He wasn't?"

"Nope." I grabbed the back of a chair to steady myself as I pulled off my boots. "About half of them skipped out, now that…now that there's no instructor."

"But Kevin said he would be there." She pushed her bowl away, looking more worried than suspicious now.

"Maybe he decided to make better use of his time by working on the ship instead."

Josie gave me a halfhearted smile. "Yeah, maybe." She picked up her spoon again and swirled it in her bowl. "So, do they have a new instructor assigned yet, or do you think they'll end up dropping the class?"

I walked around the counter and folded my arms over the opposite side with a miserable sigh. "Grace thinks I should teach it."

"Are you going to?" she asked.

"I don't think so. I'm in over my head as it is."

"It's only one class, and it's something other reapers could really benefit from right now."

I rested my chin in my hand and chewed on a fingernail. "I know, but I just don't think I'm up to it. There's so much in my life already that I'm struggling to manage."

"True." She paused to drink the milk in her bowl. "But there's no one else who could teach this class as well as you. Sometimes, the greater good outweighs the inconvenience."

"Do you think the inconvenience of Kevin and the Posy Unit is resulting in some greater good?"

Josie looked affronted. "You think Kevin is an inconvenience?"

"You know I didn't mean it that way."

"Do you think I requested a transfer to the Posy Unit for your sake? No. I did it for Kevin. *Someone* needed to be around to pick up the slack in his training."

I wasn't sure whether to be ashamed or insulted. "I didn't ask for an apprentice."

"Neither did Saul, but he still made sure you were trained properly."

"Don't bring him into this."

Josie tilted her chin up at me. "Kevin didn't ask for a shitty mentor either. You call him an inconvenience, but *I'm* the one taking care of most of his training. God, Lana. It's not always about you."

Her words hit me like a brick. I had only been joking. Hadn't I? But the truth behind it, however small, was undeniable. I *was* a shitty mentor. Even after I'd taken the mentoring course and knew all the right things I should have been doing, I wasn't doing them. Josie was. And I was taking her for granted.

"I'm sorry," I said quietly.

Her scowl softened with a hint of remorse. "Yeah, me too." She stood and fetched her jacket from the coat closet. "I'm going to check on Kevin. Sometimes, he forgets to eat when he's working on the ship."

After Josie had left, I curled up in bed with the hounds, but I couldn't sleep. My mind kept searching for the greater good in everything, and it kept coming up short.

Kevin was racking up the credentials by being my apprentice, especially as the only apprentice on a specialty unit, but did that make up for the half-assed training he was receiving? He had signed up for the demon defense course because he didn't trust that I could *or would* teach him what I'd learned from Bub. He knew I'd be substituting tonight, but he hadn't even bothered to show.

The Posy Unit was a mess in itself. Sure, it was functioning well enough, but not by any miracle on my part. I was captain for one reason: to find a replacement soul for the Throne of Eternity. I'd accomplished that task, but now I was stuck with a job that I was grossly underqualified for. My head was above water, but just barely. And the replacement soul I'd found had been installed without Grim's knowledge or permission. If my involvement came to light, where was the greater good in that?

CHAPTER TWENTY-TWO

"A man always has two reasons for doing anything:
a good reason and the real reason."
—J. P. Morgan

Around five in the morning, I woke to pounding on my bed-room door. The hounds both stirred and grunted in their sleep as I slipped out from between them and answered the knock.

Josie stood in the hallway, still in her pajamas, her arms folded tightly across her chest. "Kevin wasn't at the ship, and he never came home."

"What?" I swallowed a yawn and blinked at her. "Are you sure he wasn't working on the new cabin?"

"I checked the *whole* ship." She rubbed her temples. "He's not answering his phone either. Something's happened to him." She took a shuddering breath and folded her hands to-gether under her chin. "Please. *Please.* Help me find him."

"Of course. I'll talk to Grim first thing. Maybe he'll know something. Have you talked to Jenni?"

"She already left for the office. She's been going in ear-lier."

"Right."

I hadn't shared morning coffee with Jenni since the incident with Bub. I wasn't sure if her earlier hours were more to avoid me or because Grim was getting more desperate to find Hypnos.

Josie took a deep breath and pressed her hands over her eyes as if she might have a meltdown any second. I wasn't used to seeing her this way. It tugged at my own misery that I'd been trying so hard to kick. I shifted uncomfortably, not knowing what to do with myself.

"We'll find him. Grab your bow, take the hounds, and meet me on the ship."

She nodded and hurried off to her room while I scrambled around, throwing on jeans and a tee shirt. Even though they had been a gift from Bub, I'd kept the throwing stars. He'd set me back enough. I wouldn't hinder myself anymore on his behalf. I strapped the stars around my thigh and secured my axe across my back before pulling my robe on over everything. Then I stuffed my feet into a pair of old boots and tucked in my knives and angelica mace. I was leaving nothing to chance today.

Reapers Inc. was almost pleasant at this hour in the morning. The phones were quiet, and the entire place was infused with the aroma of freshly brewed coffee. Jenni was in Grim's office when I burst through the door. They hunched over a map spread across his desk, marking it up with the help of a few compasses and rulers.

"Kevin is missing," I said as they both looked up.

Grim raised an eyebrow at me.

"Did the Nephilim Guard report any suspicious activity yesterday or last night? Is there someone we can talk to about going over the booth surveillance footage?"

Grim gave me a pitying smirk. "Do you really expect me to waste time conducting a search party for a renegade reaper just because he's your apprentice?"

My mouth moved before I could bite my tongue. "Why not? You're wasting time conducting a search party for a useless god because he's your brother."

Grim's jaw tightened as his eyes filled with black. Just like they had when he ended Miranda. "Careful, Harvey. You're opening doors you can't close."

Jenni stood tall beside him, hands folded behind her back. Her face gave away nothing, and I was left wondering if she had known all along that Grim was wasting her skills on a personal vendetta. Maybe she didn't care. He had let her run a mission for her own gain. Perhaps she felt guilty or sympathetic to his plight.

I glared at them both. "I'm taking the day off. Josie is, too. You can fuck off all you want for whomever you like. I don't care. But you won't be stopping me from doing the same."

"And if you find him with the rebels?" Jenni said. "Will you turn him over, or conveniently ignore your duty to report to your superiors?"

I gave her a poisonous smile. "Maybe I'll serve up justice on my own. That seemed to work well for you."

Jenni locked eyes with me, shooting a silent threat across the room. I didn't need to win the staring contest. I'd said my piece, and I had a mission of my own now. I turned on my heels and marched back into the lobby, snatching my soul docket from Ellen's desk and heading for the elevators.

I made it to the ship early. Josie waited on deck with the hounds, pacing back and forth with her hands pressed to her face. She paused to seize me with her watery gray eyes, tinted red from a sleepless night.

"Anything?"

I shook my head. "But you and I are taking the day off. We'll figure this out. First, I need to get these soul dockets filled in so we can get the unit taken care of."

Josie followed me back to the new cabin. When I unlocked the door and pushed it open, a sheet of paper scraped across the floor. Kevin's handwriting raced across the page as if he had written the note in haste before slipping it under the door. Josie snatched it up and read it aloud.

"*Found rebels recruiting reapers. Went with them to Summerland to find Hypnos. Give my love to Josie. —K.*" She pressed the note to her chest and closed her eyes. "That *idiot.*"

"We'll save him, then we'll kill him."

Josie nodded and gave me a strained smile. "At least we have something to go on."

"Summerland is pretty vague, but it's a start."

I filled out the soul dockets and passed them out as soon as the team arrived, skipping right over any explanation for the heavy loads and Kevin's absence. I sent Tyler with Alex and Kate, and Molly with Arden again, making a silent vow to take a more active role in the new recruits' orientation once we found our rogue teammate.

The sea was calm as we set a course for Summerland. The trip felt like it would take forever, and then it felt too short. The coast of Summerland came into view before Josie and I had anything even remotely resembling a plan. I felt useless. It wasn't like we could just come ashore and start asking the locals if they'd seen a group of rebels and reapers pass this way. Fortunately, we didn't have to attempt it.

The yacht from the abandoned resort bobbed along the far edge of Summerland's coast, lingering in the shadow of an abundant jungle. We were too far away to tell if Kevin was on board, but it was our best bet. There was still the matter of how two reapers and a pair of hellhounds were going to take on a mob of demons, but the boat couldn't hold that many. Could it?

We had just redirected our course when the sea churned and rocked us back in the wake of a whirlpool. Water funneled up like a miniature hurricane, spewing mist into the sky. From the spinning depths emerged Caim's ship, cutting off our line of sight to the yacht.

A new demon manned the helm, and my blood ignited as I recognized her. She was the one who had put her hands on Beelzebub, claiming him on the roof of the resort. She silently pointed at us, and demons fell over themselves to do her bidding.

I pulled off my robe and threw it to the deck floor, grasping my axe. Josie had her bow in hand, but she paled at the sight of the looming ship.

"There are too many." Her voice quaked.

She dropped her bow and screamed as a cannon boomed. An iron cannonball crashed through the deck railing and lodged itself in the hatch door, splintering boards up in a nest around it.

"Josie!" I shook her arm, pulling her hand away from her face. "I don't care if there are a million demons on that boat. We're not going down without a fight. Now pick up your bow and start loosing arrows."

Josie regained a shred of resolve and retrieved her bow. Her hands still shook as she reached into her quiver, but they steadied as she took aim. She hadn't let two arrows fly before Caim's ship boomed again. Louder this time.

We both held our breath, waiting to see where the cannonball would land, but there was no impact. Not even in the sea. Then, demons began to scream. Something groaned and rumbled beneath the deck of Caim's ship, and fire and smoke blasted up through the floorboards, sending flaming splinters of wood everywhere.

"Kevin." Josie pointed to the stern deck of Caim's ship as a robed figure leapt over the railing and into the sea. "No!"

She ran over to one of the tender boats hanging off the side of our ship and clawed at the ropes, frantically digging her fingers into the knots. I untied the other side, and we climbed in, quickly maneuvering the winch that lowered the boat into the water. Once down, Josie started the motor while I unhooked us from the rigging.

Caim's ship was spinning in circles, and at first, I thought it might be sinking. I hoped it was sinking, and I prayed that Bub wouldn't be there to rescue the vixen at the wheel.

Unfortunately, it was just another vortex opening in the sea. The demons were retreating back to wherever they had come from, minus Kevin. He sloshed in the waves, ghostly souls stroking his face and shoulders as he clawed at the water.

"Faster!" Josie shouted over the roar of the currents.

I lost sight of Kevin as the ship disappeared, and for a fleeting second, I was sure he had been sucked down the rebel drain and spit out to drown elsewhere. Josie slapped my arm and pointed farther out. The waves had rocked him away from us, but he was still afloat.

I stopped the boat too late, and we almost passed right by Kevin, but Josie caught his arm, dragging him along until we came to a more complete stop. Once she'd hauled him onto the boat, her face flushed, and her eyes brimmed with tears.

"What's *wrong* with you?" She hardly gave him the chance to catch his breath before she attacked him, slapping his chest and arms with both hands as she cried.

Kevin shrank away from her, choking up water and bile. "I know where Hypnos is," he said, slopping his hair back out of his eyes. "I know where the mobile base is. I know it *all*," he rasped, smiling victoriously under Josie's assault.

He finally tucked her arms against his chest and pulled her into a suffocating hug, peppering her face with kisses as his breath returned to him.

"We need to go," I said, turning the tender boat around.

The yacht was still bobbing along the coast. A few demon faces peered over the bow, assessing us like prey. Beelzebub was among them. He could have flown to Kevin's aid, but he had been content to watch him drown. My heart reeled as I accelerated toward the ship, trying to put as much distance between us as possible.

CHAPTER TWENTY-THREE

Back at Reapers Inc., we huddled in Grim's office and listened to Kevin relay the information he had gathered during his sleepover with the enemy. I kept waiting to hear Bub's name pop up, but as far as I could tell, Kevin hadn't encountered him. There was disappointment and relief all tangled together at that, and I didn't know what to make of any of it.

Jenni was immediately ready to plan a mission, and it sounded like the rest of us might be off the hook. Which was fine with me.

"No," Grim said, silencing Jenni's spiel about careful planning. "No. We move now. No more waiting. They'll move their base again if we hesitate."

Jenni gave the rest of us a cautious frown. "Sir, are you sure you're not letting your emotional attachment to this mission cloud your judgment?"

The throbbing vein in Grim's forehead worked double-time as he glared up at Jenni. "And I'm coming with you all."

"What?" I croaked. "You all? As in, *all* of us?"

Jenni's brows knit together. "Are you sure that's wise, sir?"

Grim snarled at her. "He's my brother, and I'm coming with you," he repeated, biting out each syllable.

Jenni took a step away from him. "Fine. But I'm calling in Maalik and Gabriel. If we're going to be battling over the sea, we can't do it without them."

Grim stood, pushing his chair across the room. It smacked into the windowed wall behind his desk. "Do it. In fact, call in the Nephilim Guard while you're at it. Anyone they can spare, have them report to the harbor at once. We leave at noon."

I stood and curled my fingers at Kevin and Josie. "I think I have some extra holy water and such in my office." I needed to be away from Grim. My head was about to explode, and his delirium was only making it worse.

Ellen looked up from her desk as we exited Grim's office. She opened her mouth to say something but quickly closed it when Jenni walked out behind us. Her eyes darted back to her computer monitor and her brow crinkled as she returned to her typing.

Jenni tapped her fingers on the front desk. "I need phone numbers for Gabriel, Maalik, and the captain of the Nephilim Guard, right away."

Ellen's jaw tightened, but she quickly skimmed through her directory and scribbled the information down on a legal pad, silently sliding it across the desk to Jenni.

Jenni didn't even thank her before turning back to us. "I'll come get you once everyone has arrived and Grim is ready to go over whatever half-baked plan he comes up with."

I nodded and led Josie and Kevin down the opposite hall toward my office.

Kevin had seemed proud, almost arrogant about his little stunt. After Grim had jumped on the new insight with reckless abandon, we were all oddly downcast. We'd undertaken our fair share of dangerous missions, but we weren't usually working so blind, and for so little. I could appreciate that Hypnos was Grim's brother, but the whole situation felt wrong.

Josie's wrath resumed course when we reached my office.

"What if they'd figured out you weren't really interested in joining them? What if they asked you to do something unforgivable to prove yourself? What then?"

"And what about you?" Kevin snapped at her, dropping into one of my crummy guest chairs. "I know what Jenni's secret missions entail. I read the papers. Am I supposed to just sit around and hope you're not out there getting yourself killed? And for what? Some worthless god?"

"You told him the truth about the missions?" I gaped at Josie. Then I turned back to Kevin. "And weren't you just lecturing me on our psychopomp purpose and how we're not cut out to be soldiers?"

"So what?" Josie groaned and ran both hands over her face. "None of that matters now. We're all together, and we're all in this whether we like it or not."

I sighed. "You're right. Time to saddle up."

I opened my desk drawers and invited them to fill their pockets with all the ammunition they could manage. It wouldn't do us any good if we couldn't locate Caim's ship, but at least Grim couldn't fault us for being unprepared.

Half an hour later, Jenni came to usher us back into Grim's office. He had changed into a black robe, much like the one he wore for the Oracle Ball. It seemed too formal for battle, but for all I knew, he planned on watching from the sidelines.

Gabriel, Maalik, and Ross stood side by side before Grim's desk, their winged backs to us. As a half-blooded angel, Ross looked like the runt of the litter, even in his golden armor and crested helmet. He stole a glance behind the other two men, taking in the swell of their minor coverts and the length of their primaries. When he noticed me watching, he blushed and rustled his feathers, like checking out an angel's plumage was somehow a breach of etiquette.

Grim waited until we were circled around his desk, taking each of us in with a severe intensity in his eyes. "The rebels are getting brave. We clearly have not dealt them a blow punishing enough for them to take notice of."

The sting of his words squared my shoulders, and the angels' spines straightened, but the brunt of the insult fell on Jenni. Her face hardened, and her knuckles paled as she tightened her grasp on the sheath of her katana. Killing Caim had been a worthy victory. Grim couldn't take that away from us.

Grim pointed a finger at the window behind him, toward the harbor and sea in the distance. "They are out there, laughing at us." He slammed his fist on his desk, sending his stapler and a stack of files to the floor. "No more. Today, we will find their mobile base and destroy it. And we will bring Hypnos home."

His battle speech left a lot to be desired. The new recruits to Grim's slapdash mission traded uneasy glances. I resisted the urge to roll my eyes and followed everyone out into the lobby. Ellen stood up from her desk as we passed, circling around to grab my sleeve as I brought up the tail end of our merry band of aimless warriors.

"Warren said you had a bat problem and that this would help," she whispered, shooting a resentful look at Jenni as she pressed a small compact in my hand.

"What am I supposed to do with this?"

Ellen shrugged. "Open it, I guess. I had no idea Holly had problems with bats. Little weird if you ask me. Nasty, flying rodents."

I grinned. "I'd take that kind any day over what we're up against."

Ellen's lips pursed, but then her questioning gaze dispelled as she shook her head. "Anyway, I'd really like to talk to you when you get back." She cast another sour look at Jenni. "But not at the office or Holly House."

"Sure." I gave her a halfhearted smile as the elevators opened and I went to join the others.

Grim directed us to the travel booth across the street, and we took it to the harbor. The dock was quiet. The pounding of our boots echoed out over the sea, making us sound more like a legion, not just a handful of reapers and angels. Near the end of the pier where Jenni's vessels were docked, a dozen nephilim guards stood at attention, spears firmly at their sides, the plumes of their blue-crested helmets perfectly parallel.

The nephilim piled into Jenni's dragon boat, dropping their spears along the floorboards. They looked less anxious about the vessel than I had upon first seeing it. Of course, they could take flight if the vessel were compromised.

Grim handed Ross a slip of paper. "I hope your Latin is sharp. Recite this at the specified coordinates to open a portal. We'll meet you on the other side."

Ross nodded, but the skin around his eyes wrinkled. We were rushing into battle blind, on the whim of a mad deity. Everyone knew this was a terrible idea, but no one was ready to go head-to-head with Grim to talk him down.

I wondered at my own lack of concern. My sense of self-preservation was not at its best. The thought of running into Bub weighed on me more than anything. I couldn't understand why Grim would risk bringing me along. Maybe he was hoping it would throw Bub. Perhaps he just didn't want to share the personal details of the situation with any more allies than necessary.

Ross gave the signal, and the small fleet of nephilim opened their wings wide, letting the wind fill them. They staggered evenly, every first guard reaching higher, and every third guard kneeling, until a feathery halo formed around the boat. They thrust forward, cutting through the sea like a torpedo.

Grim turned to the rest of us and gave Jenni an uneasy look. "You're sure the submarine is our best option?"

She nodded sharply. "If we go in with nothing else, the least we should have is decent cover."

Josie didn't look as surprised about the submarine, but Kevin gaped as he squinted over the water, trying to locate the submerged vessel.

Gabriel's wings flapped sharply. "No paint this time," he growled.

Maalik folded his arms, silently agreeing.

Jenni shook her head. "It doesn't matter. The Nephilim Guard's presence will thwart any disguise efforts we could manage with so little time to prepare." She shot Grim an accusing glare.

"Let's move," he said, ignoring her jab.

Gabriel scooped me up and flew to the trunk of the submarine, quickly circling back to grab Josie while Maalik took care of Grim and Jenni. When the six of us were secure in the belly of the machine, Grim looked around the observation room, a doubtful expression creasing his face.

"How thick is this glass?" he asked.

"I've taken the sub out plenty of times. This is an infallible design," Jenni snapped.

"Even against water sirens?" I raised an eyebrow.

Jenni hesitated. "I don't know."

"I've seen them on Caim's ship, and they're more capable in the mortal seas without the tangled bodies of lethargic souls to slow them."

We all looked to Grim and waited while he worked through some inner debate.

"Once we make it through to the mortal sea, we'll be able to travel by coin back to the harbor should this vessel fail," he said.

Jenni nodded. "Just to be clear, though, my transport is covered under company liability insurance if anything *does* happen. Right?"

Grim sighed. "Of course. Now, let's go. We're wasting time."

Jenni ducked into the navigation chamber, and we were soon on our way. The Nephilim Guard had a head start, but the submarine was faster. We would reach the coordinates first. The true test of Grim's sanity would be whether or not he waited for the Guard or demanded that we forge ahead on to the mortal realm and the unknown horrors waiting within it without them. On to Bub, so the Lord of the Flies could have another go at destroying what was left of me.

As the submarine sank deeper into the heart of the sea, the outlines of the souls became more pronounced beyond the bubbled viewing window.

Kevin pressed his hands and face against the glass, staring wide-eyed in wonder. "They nearly drowned me when I jumped from Caim's ship," he said calmly as if it hadn't been intentional and he didn't hold it against them.

Josie frowned and reached for his shoulder, pulling him back a step, away from the fate she had almost lost him to.

When we arrived at the coordinates, Jenni used the periscope to check for rebel vessels along the coast. It bothered me that Seth was recruiting more heavily from Summerland. It had been my favorite afterlife to vacation in, but they did have more reason than most to jump the fence.

The mashup of extinct faiths that crowded together in the pagan territory seemed to get along well enough, but their sliver of land was eroding away more each year. Faith was not as diverse as it had once been, and the new gods in charge did not share well. It was the reason so many of the older deities had left their homelands. Most had settled in Limbo City, like Athena, Artemis, and the Muses, looking for work in the new world. And some had done the unthinkable and allowed the Fates to recycle their essence back into the mortal realm they had spawned from.

"The guards are approaching." Josie joined us in the observation room.

"Good." Grim stood and walked up to the window, rubbing his hands together as he closed his eyes. Apparently, he didn't require a spelled slip of paper to get to the other side from the middle of the sea. It made me wonder if Khadija had instilled that same ability in me.

Grim's aura seemed to thicken as if it were reaching out to encompass the entire submarine. The dusty computers along the ledge of the viewing room buzzed, their screens crackling from the buildup of static electricity. The souls outside the window arched away, their ghostly mouths drawing open in silent screams. We were left alone in the dark water.

Grim's voice came out in a steady chant. "*Patefacio porta in mortalis altum.*"

The spell was different from the one he'd given me over the summer to harvest a tsunami boating accident. I repeated the words in my mind, trying to retain the spell so I could look it up and experiment with it later.

Beyond the viewing glass, a green halo of light spread open. It widened and wrapped itself around the sub, swallowing us in darkness.

The mortal sea was full of life. A bloom of jellyfish moved out of our path, and a squid darted past the window, seizing a fish with its tentacles. It dug its beak into the scaly flesh, watching us with keen eyes.

I'd seen the mortal sea from the surface, but I'd only had a glimpse from below when a siren had tried to drown me. The memory sent a jolt of panic through me, and I looked deeper into the water, trying to sense any perilous movement.

Grim's eyes narrowed suspiciously too. "Take us to the surface," he ordered Jenni.

A tense silence filled the submarine. This battle had more on the line than those before it. Grim had left his shining tower. If he lived to tell about this day, it would be spit in Seth's face. The Egyptian leader of the rebel forces had not been seen since I'd outed him, forcing him to forfeit his position on the council.

Gloating privileges aside, Grim's actions could also be seen as recognition of the rebels' progress—as confirmation that we were, indeed, at war with them. Even if we were victorious today, we would be losing something greater. The illusion of peace. The comfort of our denial.

Ross met us at the surface as we emerged from the trunk of the submarine. A third of the nephilim guards were missing.

Ross updated Grim as we boarded the dragon boat. "I've sent eyes in every direction to locate the rebel base."

He held his hand out to Jenni to help her board, but she brushed past him, making the leap for herself. I was less proud, letting him guide me over the gunwale. Once I'd found my sea legs, I repositioned my axe, letting it hang over my robe and across my chest, the thick, double-headed blade settling against my knee.

A moment later, the scoping guards returned. The first landed beside Ross, throwing him a quick salute as he caught his breath. "We're just south of the enemy vessel."

Ross frowned and turned to the other three guards, but they shook their heads. He turned back to the first. "Only one?"

The guard nodded.

Grim pulled a scythe from under his robe and pointed it north. "Then we attack swiftly before their allies return."

Ross pounded the end of his spear on the boat floor, calling his men to attention. "First quadrant, head far north over cloud." Three of the nephilim took flight, spears held against their chest plates. "Second to the east. Third to the west. The fourth will come in last with me, providing a defensive line for Grim—"

"You will not keep me from this battle." Grim's voice was soft, but the darkness of it pooled around him, engulfing us in his quiet rage. His eyes had gone full black.

"Sir?" Ross took a careful step back, pushing the rest of us farther down the hull toward the bow.

Grim hunched over one of the stern seats, curling his head between his knees. A roar boiled up from him, growing louder as his robe ripped open across his back. Bones pressed through his pale flesh, moving in a short, aggressive rhythm like skeletal pistons. The skin thinned and tore, shredding into a wet mess as a pair of black wings sprang forth, raining blood and sinew over Grim, the boat, and the sea.

Gabriel, Maalik, and the rest of the nephilim lifted into the air, hovering just over the water. Those of us without wings huddled farther toward the back of the boat, not bothering to hide our alarm.

Grim uncurled his body, pulling himself upright. His robe lay shredded at his feet, leaving him in a pair of black slacks and combat boots. His barreled chest was pale and untouched by his blood-fused evolution. Blue veins throbbed across his body, in the bends of his elbows, and over his alien face, holding unblinking, black eyes. His wings stretched out fully, fanning in slow circles. Blood dripped from his feathers. "No more talking."

None of us had the nerve to argue. I think at that moment, we were all just glad that he was on our side.

Grim picked up his scythe and stepped up onto the gunwale, diving off the side of the boat. His wet wings hissed as they lifted him into the sky. Maalik and Ross darted after him, while Gabriel dove down to collect me in his arms.

The three remaining guards carried Jenni, Josie, and Kevin. Their smaller wings struggled with the added weight. Gabriel waited for them, though he glanced ahead anxiously, trying to keep Grim and the others in sight.

I pressed my head into his neck. "No dropping me on hellcats this time. Let the guards take care of the dirty work."

Gabriel gave me a hollow smile that didn't reach his eyes. His words came out in a strained whisper. "I think Grim's gone off the deep end. Don't overextend yourself today. Try not to draw too much attention. If Grim's recklessness results in his death, we're retreating. Do you understand?" He looked down at me, boring his blue eyes into mine. "This could all go very badly, very fast. *You* are my only priority."

My stomach knotted. "Maalik—"

"Screw Maalik." He pulled me tight against his chest. "I've had your back long before he came into the picture."

I squeezed Gabriel's arm. "I'll be careful."

Up ahead, Caim's ship cut into the horizon. The boat had definitely seen better days. The explosion Kevin had set off with their gunpowder supply had ripped boards loose along the hull. All the gun ports were charred around the edges like the thing had breathed fire for some time after its last retreat. Blood stained the deck floor around the masts where merry satyrs and succubi had once danced.

The demons on board were still licking their wounds. Some of the more carnivorous species were busy picking the bones of their fallen comrades, while the injured watched on in horror, trying their best to hide any signs of weakness.

A trumpet sounded in the distance, just as the first three quadrants of nephilim descended on the ship. Grim touched down a moment later. Demons cowered in his presence. A brave creature made a leap for him, backpedaling too late as Grim's hand closed around his skull, crushing it like rotten fruit.

Gabriel's grip on me tightened.

I patted his arm. "Something tells me we won't be the ones retreating today."

Gabriel shivered. "I am become Death, the destroyer of worlds."

"Game face, Gabriel. Game face." My hands tightened around the handle of my axe.

The nephilim carrying the other reapers quickened their pace as we drew closer. Their faces flushed in strain as they searched the ship deck, looking for a secluded spot to land.

The battle was in full throe. Two nephilim stabbed their spears at a hellcat on the forecastle deck, while another staved off a trident-wielding demon. Ross tried to flank Grim, but soon caught the attention of a siren. He covered his ears as she perched on the railing of the quarterdeck and began to sing.

I glanced over at Kevin. He shuddered and closed his eyes.

When we touched down on the stern deck, he quickly pressed a set of earplugs into his ears. He didn't go anywhere without them these days.

The nephilim guards who had helped deliver us didn't waste any time. They were still gasping to catch their breath as they slipped down to the main deck to join the fight. We were close behind them.

A hiss from the quarterdeck snapped my neck around. The succubus I'd seen with Bub was at the wheel, trying to turn the ship around. I broke from the pack to go after her.

It would have been easy to convince myself that the assault was to keep her from seeking out reinforcements. But I wasn't looking for easy today. However irrational it might have been, in my mind, she had taken Bub from me. She'd lured him to the dark side. She had put a spell on him, and I was going to break it. Along with her face.

My axe came down on the helm wheel, taking off her pinky as the blade cut through the felloes and splintered the spokes, rendering the wheel useless.

The demon tramp let out a shriek of rage and cradled her hand to her chest. She backed away from me and climbed up the outer wall of the navigation room. When she reached the edge of the roof, she turned and used the wall as a springboard to launch herself at me. I held my axe out with both hands, catching her across the chest and one shoulder as her hands found my neck. Claws scratched across my throat, and blood gushed from her pinkyless hand, running down my collarbone in a burning line.

Jenni stepped in behind her and smashed a vial of holy water across the demon's naked back. The hag let go, hissing as she hit the deck floor, writhing and arching in pain.

My breath rasped as I lifted my axe with both hands. I brought it down like a lumberjack, but not quickly enough. The demon's eyes opened wide, and she rolled away, under the railing and onto the main deck, disappearing into the battle.

My axe sank through the deck boards, and my anger fizzled out in a heaving moan.

"Lana!" Gabriel landed behind me and wrapped his hands around the horns of a satyr I hadn't noticed creeping up on me. He smashed the creature's head into the railing and scowled. "I told you not to draw attention."

I turned away from him and scanned the main deck, searching for my lost quarry through the carnage. A hellcat sprang onto the back of a nephilim, pinning him to the floor as it tore off his wings with its teeth. The guard cried out, desperately reaching for his spear. Before he could grab it, the hellcat crunched down on the back of his neck and tossed him overboard.

The splash was followed by the bellow of a conch horn. Grim walked to the edge of the deck to look down at the new arrivals.

"Hear me, o' Death." Eurynome rose up on the back of her stationary wave. A throne of shells cupped her, and a coral crown graced her golden locks. "Well, well. Out of hiding and out of the closet, all in one day," she cooed and tapped her delicate fingers across the armrests of her throne.

Grim took her in with a blank expression.

The look painted a pout on Eurynome's face. "You know, I had originally suggested snagging your mother. But she's a slippery thing, dear Nyxie."

Grim's head tilted slightly, and he blinked his wide, black eyes at her. From Eurynome's angle, she couldn't see the abandoned spear he was slipping his boot under. He kicked it upward and caught it one-handed before hurling it over the sea.

Eurynome gasped as the spear zipped past her and sank into the eye of a siren in the water behind her. The mermaid's wail ripped through my skull. I pressed my hands over my ears until the noise bubbled away beneath the sea.

"Lorelei!" Eurynome roared. "Invite our friends to this side."

A familiar siren swam over to the bloodstained water and smiled up at Kevin before turning her back. Her hands glowed as she pressed them together and parted them beneath the water. The light swerved away from her, and the sea sparkled as it rippled open, spawning a small whirlpool. The yacht rose in its center with Bub at the helm. His eyes found mine, and all the air left my lungs.

The battle on the ship resumed more fiercely. The demons found their second wind now that Eurynome and Beelzebub's minions had joined the fight.

"You!" Josie marched past me, pointing her finger at one of the nephilim guards as he pulled his spear from the head of a fallen demon. When the guard noticed her, she turned her finger toward the yacht. "Take me there."

The guard lifted her up and took off.

"Josie!" I ran to the ship railing, screaming after her, but I was too late.

Gabriel caught me as I turned around.

"You have to take me after her," I begged.

"No." He shook my arms. "Absolutely not. You're not ready to face off with him."

"What about Josie?" I dug my nails into his arms.

"I'm your guardian angel, not hers."

I jerked my arms away from his and picked up my axe. I had to do something. Anything.

The succubus I'd harvested a finger from glared at me from the bow of the ship. I locked my sights on her and leapt over the railing, landing hard in a crouched position. The blood-soaked boards creaked from the impact.

When I looked up, the hag had moved. I caught a glimpse of her tangled hair as she disappeared around the forecastle. I stalked her slowly, keeping a wary eye on the demons surrounding me. I paused to gut a hellcat advancing on a pair of guards. Kevin shouted to me, and I tossed him my spare can of angelica mace.

Halfway across the deck, Grim stumbled across my path. Sharur, the smasher of thousands, ground against his scythe. My thigh warmed, and I remembered Warren's compact in my pocket. I dug it out and popped open the lid one-handed. A flashing red dart lifted out of the tin. It began to beep and made a beeline for the enchanted mace.

"Everyone down!"

The second the dart reached the weapon, it exploded. A firework blossom of splinters and metal shards rained down on the battle. Either Warren hadn't explained the device to Ellen, or Ellen hadn't been paying attention. It didn't matter. Someone was going to get the third degree over this one, and it wouldn't be me.

When I finally made my way to the front of the ship, the succubus was gone. I climbed up to the forecastle deck and took a quick look around. A splinter of wood hit the deck beside me, and I glanced up. She was halfway up the foremast, leaving a bloody trail along the rough wood. She paused to catch her breath and flexed her injured hand as she glared down at me.

A cry from across the sea caught both of our attentions. Josie stood on the deck of the yacht, firing arrow after arrow at the crew. Bub was gone, and my entire body froze in anguish. *Did she shoot him? Was he dead?* Then a swarm of flies came into focus, buzzing across the water, heading straight for me. *No.* Heading straight for the succubus.

My concern for Bub was replaced by fury. I glared up at the demon and tore off my robe, snatching two of the throwing stars from the strap around my thigh. Cruel vengeance seared through me, and it felt so much better than the heartache I'd been battling.

I hurried down to the main deck, ignoring the demons and guards as I ran past them. Then I turned and took aim. The first star struck the demon's lower back. She cried out and twisted around, reaching for the source of her pain, leaving herself wide-open. The second star sank into the hollow of her throat.

She let go of the mast and fell, but before she hit the deck floor, Bub arrived, materializing from his swarm of flies. He caught her in a gentle embrace, one hand under her knees and the other around her back. My blood boiled as I watched her bloody hand wrap around his shoulder. Her eyes fluttered open and scanned the deck until she found me. Even with a throwing star stuck in her throat, she smiled.

Bub didn't look back. He shifted into his swarm and took flight, carrying the succubus back toward the yacht where Josie was battling alone now. I didn't know whether her nephilim companion had abandoned her, or if he'd been taken down by the rebels. At any rate, she was losing steam.

The demons had thinned, but there were still quite a few left. Some had retreated below deck, and some hid along the aft end of the yacht behind the wheelhouse, occasionally making a run at her before she filled them with arrows. The ones who could fly thought they could escape her wrath, but she had shot most of them down too—aside from Bub in his buggy form.

Josie watched Bub's swarm approach and took aim at the succubus. I held my breath, hoping her arrow would find its mark. Neither of us noticed the siren until she was at Josie's back.

Lorelei snatched Josie's quiver, wrenching her off her feet. The back of my friend's head smacked the center of the siren's naked chest, and Lorelei held Josie there, weaving her scaly fingers through Josie's hair, snaking them around the sides of her face. I forgot how to swallow. I forgot how to breathe.

It seemed a blithe and almost intimate gesture at first, like a lover's caress. The siren's eyes had a seductive tint to them as they grazed past me, finding their way to Kevin. When she had his full attention, she dug her fingers into Josie's eyes, pressing them knuckle-deep into the sockets.

Josie's scream bled into Kevin's and my own, but hers was cut short as the siren twisted her head to the side, snapping her neck.

Everything slowed to a painful crawl. All except for the murderous pulse pounding behind my eyes. I didn't have time to react. Kevin's hand was stretched out before him. His voice raged over the wind, booming through it like thunder.

"*SANCTUS INCENDIA.*"

The fire shot forth from his hand like a blow torch, leaving in a long, snaking stream with a mind and mission of its own. It seared through the air like a comet, burning brighter as it reached the yacht. The siren forgot her victory and turned away, screaming as she ran up the open bow. She never made it to the water.

Kevin's fire pierced her backside and filled her with angry, red light. Her skin cooked to her ribcage, drying taut against the bones before turning black and flaking off. Her screams hung in the air until I wasn't sure if the high-pitched shriek was a residual echo on the sea, or if it was all in my head, my subconscious breaking on some level I couldn't grasp.

Eurynome's song carried over the water, turning the heads of her sirens in unison. The few battling on the deck of the flaming ship retreated, diving into the sea. They were abandoning the demons and fleeing under the waves. Eurynome turned her eyes up to Grim, glaring her contempt over the cresting sea foam as it swallowed her.

Bub materialized on the yacht and held the succubus to his chest as he shouted to a demon below deck. The yacht motor roared to life. A satyr ran up to the bow and scooped up Josie's body, flinging it over the edge and into the sea. A horn blasted from the yacht's wheelhouse, calling out to the demons on Caim's ship to retreat. The rebels had lost this battle.

The remaining rebels on the ship climbed onto the backs of hellcats. Some latched on to the arms and legs of winged demons as they fled. A few dropped into the sea and attempted to swim the distance. Bub didn't wait. The nephilim prepared to give chase, but Grim stilled them as the yacht sped off. Instead, he pointed to the few demons treading water and ordered the guards to take no prisoners.

When the yacht disappeared on the horizon, my knees gave out, and I fell to the deck floor, clutching my fist over my heaving chest. Gabriel knelt beside me and placed a hand on my back. I was too spent to shake him off.

"Go get her body," I said, rocking myself against the pain and rage coursing through me.

Kevin sat on the other end of the deck with his back pressed against the lower cabin wall. His blood-spattered face was empty, completely drained of emotion. The hand he had spelled with was lying palm up on the deck, scorched black all the way out to his blistered fingertips.

The Nephilim Guard searched Caim's ship and found Hypnos in a secluded cabin, tucked inside a lushly lined coffin. When Grim woke him, their reunion clouded the ship in a haze of peaceful silence. Death had been sated, and we were all tired.

Gabriel laid Josie's body in the emptied coffin, covering her ruined eyes with two coins and folding her hands over her bow. Kevin spent the longest time standing over her, the dead emptiness never lifting from his face. Jenni and I watched over him, keeping our distance and avoiding looking at each other.

Dusk was falling on the mortal realm. The sun touched the horizon, lighting up the sky in an array of vibrant pinks and oranges. They reflected off the water and melted into each other. It was a beautiful end to an ugly day.

Ross ordered the nephilim to retrieve the dragon boat and the submarine. When all three vessels were gathered, we went our separate ways. Jenni and Maalik took the submarine, and Kevin, Gabriel, and I loaded into the dragon boat with Josie's coffin. Ross and the nephilim guards went with Grim to take Hypnos back to his cave before returning to the city.

Grim was keeping the ship as a trophy, hoping it would serve as a warning to those who opposed the council. He opened a portal big enough for all three vessels to pass through, and we left the sunset and the blood-tinged waters behind.

CHAPTER TWENTY-FOUR

*"If you tell a lie long enough, people will think it's the truth.
And that is how religion began."*
—Rodolfo Perez

When we docked at the harbor, Gabriel and Maalik took Josie's coffin to Reapers Inc. where it would stay until they discussed how to proceed with Grim. Kevin wanted to go with them, but Jenni stopped him, pointing out the damage to his hand. He didn't seem concerned, but she insisted on seeing him to Meng Po's. I should have gone with them. Instead, I coined off from the harbor.

I had no business being in Tartarus. Everything I loved there was ruined. It seemed so stupid now how I had associated such joy with a hell region.

The summer manor was nothing more than a pile of rubble—aside from a few beams that refused to fall—so I took the mountain trail up to the viewing ledge with the telescope. No one else knew about it, so it had been left undisturbed.

I twisted the scope around and pointed it toward the poppy fields that surrounded Hypnos's cave. Caim's conquered ship was docked in a port off the Lethe, the river of forgetfulness. I should have gone with them. Maybe a dip in the river would cure all that ailed me.

This was the part where I was supposed to be cheering a victory song and celebrating at Purgatory Lounge with my comrades. We'd saved the day. All was right in the afterlife again, only…not really. I guess that's why I was moping in Tartarus instead.

The wind around the desert mountain picked up, and a soft buzzing grew louder. Terror flickered through me. I let go of the telescope and stepped back into the shadow of the mountain.

And then he was on the ledge with me. Bub stood a few feet away, gazing up at the starry sky. He was in his black commando uniform. He didn't look like the man I had fallen for and made love to on an old houseboat that was nothing but charred driftwood now.

His eyes glazed over as he turned them to me. The silence crackled between us like static, as if he might zap and fade away if I blinked or came too close. I had so many questions. He was alone tonight. This was my moment, and I had a feeling it would be the only one I got.

Tears burned my eyes. I closed the distance between us and slammed my fists into his chest. He let me, taking the abuse with defeat smeared across his face.

"Why?" I sobbed, not caring how hysterical I sounded.

This was what I had longed for from the second I'd seen him on that rooftop. A moment alone so I could have answers, like that could somehow make everything okay again. I had some stupidly smooth monolog all worked out in my head, courtesy of too many restless nights, but it was all forgotten now that he was here.

"I hate you." It was all I could manage. "God, I hate you so much." My fists finally tired and rested against his chest, bruised and throbbing.

"I know." Beelzebub ran his fingers over my cheeks, wiping away tears that just kept flowing. "I know," he whispered.

I wasn't sure who moved first, but our mouths were suddenly one. Teeth scraped on lips and tongues. Our lungs heaved in time with one another. And then we were on the ground, peeling off clothes and becoming impossibly tangled.

Beelzebub was crying now, too. Heavy, endless tears leaked from his eyes and splashed onto my face. They trailed their way to my lips, leaving a bitter, sulfuric aftertaste. Each time he pressed into me felt like an apology that I couldn't accept, but every time he drew away, I pulled him back to me. I hated him for it, but I hated myself more.

This was goodbye, and we both knew it.

Our finish was anticlimactic. I rolled out from under him, turning away and covering my face. Bub's breath was hoarse across the base of my neck. His fingertips trembled as he slowly ran them down my back.

"Why?" I could barely whisper.

Bub's hand stopped moving. "I had to. We needed a spy among the rebels."

I gasped and turned back to him, tucking my face into his neck. "You asshole. Why didn't you tell me before?"

Bub nuzzled his face in my hair and breathed deeply. "I'm not supposed to be telling you now. Cindy would kill me. Then she'd kill you. No one else knows. We can't risk exposure if the rebels have a mole on our side."

"You could have told *me* sooner."

"But your scorned lover act wouldn't have been half as convincing," he said.

"I'm still scorned." I pressed my cheek against his shoulder.

"I know. I'm sorry."

"This is really it, isn't it?" My voice cracked as the tears crept back into my eyes.

For a second, everything had felt like it might get better. Bub still loved me. He was just pretending to be an evil bastard. The problem was, he had to keep pretending. That clearly wasn't going to afford him much time for me.

Bub took my shoulders and pulled away so he could look me in the eyes. "It's not forever. Just until Seth is within reach. Once we take him out, his army will fall."

"How long?" I asked.

"I don't know."

"And until then?"

He pulled me back against his chest. "We remember this moment, right now, and we take comfort in it. For the greater good."

I swallowed back a sob as I remembered Josie's case for the greater good. I wanted to believe that's what we were working toward. That all of this hurt and anger and loss would somehow pay off in the long run.

Bub and I lay quietly under the stars, watching them migrate across the sky, stealing time from us. I wanted to make rash suggestions, like how we could find another houseboat and run off to the mortal realm together, never to be seen again. But the fact that he had sacrificed our relationship for the council, for the *greater good,* made me realize that it was useless. And it made me feel rotten and selfish for wanting to discredit the other sacrifices he'd made. The sacrifices *everyone else* had made. It couldn't all be for nothing.

I lay perfectly still, nestled in against him, trying to freeze the moment. But, eventually, Bub stirred.

"I have to go. I've been gone too long as it is."

I laced my fingers with his and squeezed. "When will I see you again?"

Bub rubbed a patch of dirt from my shoulder and gave me a gentle smile. "I don't know." He tilted my chin up with his fingers. "But you *will* see me again. I promise." He put his mouth to mine, and his breath danced across my lips, tickling its way down my jaw and neck.

I closed my eyes halfway through the kiss, melting into it. Tears soaked through my lashes, and when I opened my eyes, Bub was gone.

I didn't want to leave the ledge. If I left, it would be as if it had never happened. It was like I had dreamed it all, just a hopeful trick my mind had concocted now that I was losing it. I couldn't let it be that.

I found my clothes and put them back on, feeling vulnerable now that I was alone. Then I picked up a sharp rock and sliced it across the inside of my hand. It wasn't a deep wound, but it produced enough blood to coat my palm and fingers.

I found a secluded dip in the mountainside, leading into a shallow cave. There I pressed my hand to a smooth span of rock wall, leaving my mark, evidence of the night. Bub could think on the moment all he wanted. I needed something real. I needed a sign. And now I had one.

I returned to the ledge and looked over the lip. Darkness pooled at the base of the mountain, hiding the desert floor. The climb up had been painstaking and long, but the fall was always easy. Always fast.

I held my coin tightly, and my breath even tighter as I turned and fell from the ledge. Stale adrenaline tingled through my limbs. The last time I had jumped from this point, Bub had caught me. It had been a ridiculous gesture of my trust in him. He wouldn't be catching me this time.

I waited until the last moment and then rolled my coin.

CHAPTER TWENTY-FIVE

"What we have done for ourselves alone dies with us; what we have done for others and the world remains and is immortal."
—*Albert Pike*

I didn't see much of Kevin the rest of the week. He took some time off and spent most of it in his room. I wanted to stay home and grieve with him, but I didn't have that luxury. The unit was hurting, and I couldn't imagine how it would have fared without the two new reapers. No one complained about the extra workload while Kevin was gone.

After Grim had Josie cremated and her ashes sealed in a memorial bench at the park, Kevin finally left the condo long enough to walk the hounds over for a visit. He skipped the memorial service, though. I went with Jenni.

Jenni didn't have much to say about Josie, but she did start having coffee with me in the mornings again. I wasn't sure if it was to soothe herself or me, but either way, I'd take it.

Bub's confession had salvaged a piece of me, and the small bit of hope I felt made Josie's death seem that much worse. I felt guilty for having any capacity for happiness whatsoever. I felt so guilt-ridden, in fact, that come Monday night, I found myself sitting in front of Grace Adaline's desk.

"You're sure?" Grace tilted her head down to look at me over the top of her glasses, concern and skepticism filling her eyes.

I cleared my throat and folded my hands over my knee. "I know how important this course is—now more than ever. I think I could manage taking it on *if* you allow me an assistant."

Grace raised an eyebrow. "Did you have someone in mind?"

A small smile pulled up the corners of my mouth as I redefined the greater good for myself. "I do."

Jack had never been to the Reaper Academy before. He stood at the front of the empty classroom and adjusted his tie for the hundredth time.

"You'll do fine." I dusted a sprinkle of chalk from his sleeve.

Jackson Bifrons Leonard Melchom was written across the blackboard in Jack's impeccable cursive.

"You know," Jack said, shaking his finger at the board. "At one time, it was considered quite taboo to give away one's true name. The mortals were especially malicious with their dark arts in the Middle Ages. We had to put an end to it right quick."

I grinned. "I just meant for you to write your first name. Or whatever you'd like the students to call you."

"Oh." Jack's shoulders perked in understanding. He snatched up the eraser and quickly wiped away the last three names, leaving only Jackson. He frowned a moment before adding *Mr.* before it. "That should do."

The first students trickled in, pausing as their gazes fell on Jack. They assessed his horns first, taking in the bandages on the one he had busted. It was healing nicely, but I had convinced him to milk the injury a bit longer for the sake of sympathy. And it worked. The students slowly took their seats.

Jack folded his arms behind his back and smiled, his proud posture conforming to the lines of his crisp suit. Some of the students even smiled back at him. Demon relations in the city might not have been at their best, but they were certainly never going to improve until we did something about it. There was greater good to be done here.

When the bell rang, I was disappointed to see that Kevin hadn't shown. Lacy Irman had decided to make an appearance, even though she considered me inadequate. She folded her arms and glared from me to Jack.

"Good evening." I stood and walked around to the front of the desk. "First, I'd like to update you all on the status of this class. It will be moving forward as planned, but I'll be taking over as the professor."

"Can we get our money back if we drop it now?" Lacy shouted from the back row.

I ground my teeth together and smiled at her. "This is only the third class period. Even if there hadn't been a change in professor, you would still be within the grace period to drop the class."

Lacy smirked and whispered something to a student next to her. I looked away and went on with my lesson plan for the evening.

"I'll be teaching this class with the aid of Mr. Jackson, who was responsible for a good deal of my training—"

"Wasn't he also responsible for washing your rebel boyfriend's underwear?" Lacy laughed at her own joke, and a few students joined her.

Jack's cheery expression deflated, and my hand was in the air before I knew what I was doing.

"*Sanctus Incendia.*"

I didn't have to say it loudly. There was enough force behind my words to splinter her desk in half with a spear of flames. Lacy tumbled from her chair into a pile of knees and elbows. She crawled backward until she hit the wall, her glassy bug-eyes never leaving mine.

I sat on the edge of my desk and slowly crossed my legs. "If you're interested in learning demon defense, you're welcome to stay. If you're interested in running your mouth while I'm trying to teach, please remove your sorry ass from my classroom. Immediately."

Lacy picked herself up off the floor. She didn't glare or open her mouth, so I was able to deduce that she possessed at least half a brain. She quietly gathered her books, the ones that weren't smoldering in the remains of her desk, and scampered out of the room.

"Now," I said, clapping my hands together. "While Jack finds a fire extinguisher and puts out the remains of Ms. Irman's desk, I believe the rest of you have a test to take." I pulled a stack of papers out of my bag and handed them to a student in the first row. "Take one and pass them along."

The reaper nodded, keeping his eyes down as he followed my instruction.

"One last thing before you start your tests," I said, turning to walk back to my desk. "If *any* of you take the information I teach in this classroom back to the rebels, I will personally hunt you down and terminate you myself."

The classroom was silent. Every eye was on me. The threat went a long way in expelling any question about where my loyalties fell. It also demanded the respect and attention I would require in order to educate a room full of reapers in demon defense. There was no sense in taking on the task unless I planned on doing it right.

I looked up at the clock above the classroom door and nodded. "You have one hour. You may begin."

Pencils scratched across paper, and brows furled. No one spoke. No one tried to cheat.

Jack walked over to me and rested his hand on my shoulder with a smile. "You're doing well," he said softly.

After class, I took the booths to Holly House. I was so wrapped up in my thoughts that I didn't notice the hooded figure waiting across the street in front of the Little Folk Shoppe. Not until Winston shouted my name and waved to me.

"What are you doing here?" I whispered as we ducked around to the backside of the building to the secret garden spot.

Winston pinched a thick coin between his fingers. It was a deep charcoal gray like the one he'd given me before that Loki and Caim had taken.

"I have something for you." Winston held the coin out to me.

I clenched my hands into fists at my sides. "Keep it."

He shook his head. "What?"

"You watched my life fall apart from the sidelines, and you did nothing."

"I couldn't—"

"You could have *told* me!" I closed my eyes and tried to swallow back the rage building in my throat. "You could have told me, and I could have prevented it."

Winston's hand dropped, and he looked away. "Preventing those events would only have led to worse ones."

"Worse according to whom?"

He wouldn't answer.

It occurred to me—and not for the first time—that Winston hadn't replaced my coin sooner because he didn't want to deal with my pleas for help. Now that there was nothing he could do, here he was, offering me a coin as some noble gesture when we both knew the benefit was all his now.

"Keep the coin. Maalik can be your lapdog."

Winston finally looked up at me. "But you're the only one who knows about Naledi."

"And if you want to keep it that way, I suggest you leave me alone for the next century. Maalik can handle fetching your trinkets in the meantime. That is why you're trying to give me a coin now, right? Because it's clearly not so I can come to *you* for anything so trivial as a warning when my best friend is about to die or when my lover is about to turn evil."

"Lana." Shame tinted his cheeks, and he looked away again. If I was wrong, it was only by half.

"Goodbye, Winston."

I left him standing alone in the alley and headed for Holly House. The fate of Eternity didn't rest on his shoulders anymore, so I didn't see why his destiny needed to weigh on mine. I had too much on my plate as it was, and certainly not enough time to nurture a one-sided friendship.

CHAPTER TWENTY-SIX

*"The dead cannot cry out for justice.
It is a duty of the living to do so for them."*
—*Lois McMaster Bujold*

"**A**nonymous tip came in yesterday." Jenni grunted as my fist connected with her sparring pad. It was after ten, and we were the only two left at the dojo. We'd been doing this every night since Josie's memorial.

"Yeah?"

"About a nest of illegal demons camped out in the jungle off the coast of Summerland."

I slugged the sparring pad again, harder this time, pushing past the ache building in my shoulder. We were creeping up on three hours of training, but I felt like I needed another three before I'd be exhausted enough to actually sleep tonight.

Jenni rubbed the sweat from her forehead with the back of her hand. "How well do your hellhounds track?"

"Coreen, not for shit. But Saul is top-notch."

"We could use him tomorrow, then."

I nodded once and threw another punch. Something in my stomach tightened, but it was more in anticipation than dread. Distractions were getting harder to come by, and slaying demons was as good as any.

Still, my heart wavered at the thought of running into Bub. There was no way to warn him. Part of me was still furious that I'd been left in the dark, but a much larger part was swimming in euphoria over the fact that he was just playing a role. Even if that included getting chummy with a succubus I still wanted to murder. Even if it included watching as Josie was killed.

The guilt was consuming me, and I wanted to hate Bub for that. The reenactment of Josie's death that haunted my dreams almost always featured a cameo of Bub rescuing the succubus tramp. I couldn't separate the two images, and it tainted what little joy I had salvaged from the wreckage of my life.

Some nights, when I woke covered in sweat and tears, I would slip out to the harbor and coin off to Tartarus. A run up the mountain trail seemed to work the kinks out of my psyche. When I reached the telescope ledge, I'd feel my way around in the dark until I found the alcove I had branded. I'd remember the moment we shared, and I'd take comfort in it. For the greater good.

Catch up with Lana and company in…

DEATH WISH

LANA HARVEY, REAPERS INC. BOOK FIVE

Available Now in Print, eBook, and Audio!

Lana Harvey's been through hell and back.

As a reaper, it's all part of the job, but the afterlife has been more turbulent than usual. The Second War of Eternity is underway, and the streets of Limbo City are heavy with the scent of carnage and betrayal. With the recent death of a dear friend, a lover-turned-spy, and temperamental gods breathing down her neck, Lana's days seem numbered. But Eternity isn't done with her yet.

ACKNOWLEDGMENTS

2019 10-year anniversary update: I can hardly believe that Lana turns 10 this year! To celebrate, I asked Rebecca Frank to revamp the cover designs, my cousin Kaitlyn Beck to pose as Lana, my husband Paul to photograph her, and my editor Chelle Olson to clean up my early work that I heavily relied on English-savvy teacher pals to proofread back in the day. I also can't forget shout-outs to Hollie Jackson, the epic narrator who voices Lana in the audiobooks; the Four Horsemen of the Bookocalypse, my amazing critique group; and THE professor George Shelley, whose enthusiasm for Lana's world motivated me at times I'd almost given up on writing. All my gratitude to you wonderful mavens who make my books shine and my heart swell.

Original acknowledgments: I think this book was trying to kill me. Seriously. Thank goodness I had so many friends and dedicated readers to keep the fire burning. Your encouraging emails and excited reviews helped fuel this story along when I thought I'd reached my wit's end.

Special thanks is due to my critique group, the Four Horsemen of the Bookocalypse: Kory Shrum, Katie Pendleton, and Monica La Porta. Thank you for providing so much useful feedback, and for delivering it in a non-soul-crushing way. You ladies are the best! I'm looking forward to playing Cards Against Humanity with you all at RT in Dallas next year!

I would also like to thank my book club: Felicia, Kristy, Ashleigh, and Sam. Your diverse selections have brought so much unexpected delight to my shelves. I always look forward to our monthly meetings, and not just because they keep me from becoming a legit shut-in.

Huge thanks are due to my husband and son for loving me and bearing with me through yet another book; my supportive parents and siblings who inspire me with their own achievements every day; and Professor Shelley, for checking in from time to time to see what was taking Lana so long. I hope the wait was worth it.

And, finally, I would like to thank everyone who helped edit and proofread this novel. Your enthusiasm and support make all the difference in the world to me, and I can't thank you enough for saving me from embarrassing typos and grammatical missteps. All remaining errors are my own.

ABOUT THE AUTHOR

USA Today bestselling author **Angela Roquet** is a delightfully macabre weirdo. She lives in Missouri with her irresistible BFF husband, their sweet, clever son, and a majestic marshmallow of a Great Pyrenees in a house stuffed with books, toys, skulls, owls, and glitter-speckled craft supplies.

Angela is a member of the Science Fiction and Fantasy Writers Association, as well as the Four Horsemen of the Bookocalypse, her epic book critique group, where she's known as Death. When not swearing at the keyboard, she enjoys playing with her family and reading books that raise eyebrows.

You can find Angela online at **www.angelaroquet.com**

If you enjoyed this book, please leave a review or tell a friend. Your enthusiasm and support make these books possible, and it means the world to me!